HEART DOCTOR'S SUMMER REUNION

JANICE LYNN

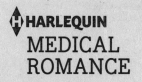

HARLEQUIN
MEDICAL
ROMANCE

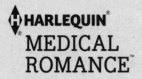

MEDICAL ROMANCE™

Recycling programs
for this product may
not exist in your area.

ISBN-13: 978-1-335-59496-9

Heart Doctor's Summer Reunion

Copyright © 2023 by Janice Lynn

For questions and comments about the quality of this book,
please contact us at CustomerService@Harlequin.com.

Harlequin Enterprises ULC
22 Adelaide St. West, 41st Floor
Toronto, Ontario M5H 4E3, Canada
www.Harlequin.com

Printed in U.S.A.

"Lottie."

Saying her name out loud had his heart hammering even faster. Maybe he'd rounded the corner and he'd been the one hit in the head. His was certainly spinning enough he'd believe something had hit him.

"Linc!" Green gaze wide, eyeing his still-raised weapon, she hugged the towel barely covering her midsection.

"What are you doing here?" they asked in unison.

Not that Linc couldn't guess. She'd returned because of Jackie's fall. Jackie hadn't mentioned Lottie's return when she'd asked him to please make sure the ambulance crew had locked up her place. Did she know her only grandchild was home? He'd thought it odd that she hadn't asked Mary Baker, her next-door neighbor and who'd taken Jackie's Carolina dog home with her the night before, but he'd agreed that he'd go by as soon as he finished sanding the bathroom walls he'd spackled earlier that week.

Lottie was back.

Linc fought to keep his eyes on her face rather than the body that had haunted his dreams for over a decade. Maybe one's first love always set the bar by which to measure all others.

Dear Reader,

I first visited Fripp Island several years ago for a writers' retreat and fell in love with the area. In this story, I mention an old research facility on Pritchard's Island. The abandoned structure always fascinated me. During the time I was writing this story, it was torn down. I imagine the next time I'm there, I'll be much like my heroine and feel nostalgia when I look at where it once proudly stood, recalling kayaking trips, picnics and exploration on Pritchard's. Of course, Lottie's memories are also filled with the perfect summer she spent falling in love with Linc Thomas.

When the health of Lottie's grandmother warrants her spending a few weeks in Fripp, Lottie is surprised that Linc lives on the island. Linc was her first love and the man she compares all others to. At eighteen, he'd broken her heart at summer's end, preferring to say goodbye than to pursue a long-distance relationship. The spark is still there, but so are the miles between their homes. After their sweet reunion, would he be willing to give long-distance love a chance this time around? Would she? Could she risk her heart knowing that he'd so easily said goodbye?

I hope you enjoy Lottie and Linc's story as much as I enjoyed writing it. I love to hear from my readers, so feel free to message me at janicemarielynn@gmail.com.

Happy reading,

Janice

USA TODAY and *Wall Street Journal* bestselling author **Janice Lynn** has a master's in nursing from Vanderbilt University and works as a nurse practitioner in a family practice. She lives in the southern United States with her Prince Charming, their children, their Maltese named Halo and a lot of unnamed dust bunnies that have moved in after she started her writing career. Readers can visit Janice via her website at janicelynn.net.

Books by Janice Lynn

Harlequin Medical Romance

A Surgeon to Heal Her Heart
Heart Surgeon to Single Dad
Friend, Fling, Forever?
A Nurse to Tame the ER Doc
The Nurse's One Night to Forever
Weekend Fling with the Surgeon
Reunited with the Heart Surgeon
The Single Mom He Can't Resist

Visit the Author Profile page
at Harlequin.com for more titles.

**Janice won the National Readers' Choice Award
for her first book,
The Doctor's Pregnancy Bombshell.**

With love to my grandmother Janie Green, who broke
her foot last summer and inspired this story.

CHAPTER ONE

FLIPPING ON THE LIGHT, Dr. Charlotte Fairwell breathed in the familiar surroundings of her grandmother's South Carolina home, a plethora of comfort, art and bright colors that all told of the sea.

Walking to the kitchen island, Lottie ran her fingers over a smooth piece of bird-shaped driftwood that her grandmother had twisted rusted wire around and mounted on a pedestal. Lottie had visited last year over the Christmas holidays, but her grandmother's artwork was constantly in flux, and she wanted to wander through the house to reconnect with every nook and cranny of the two-story home. Her red-eye flight out of Boston that morning was taking its toll, though. She'd shower, then sleep. With Gram in the hospital, the next few days weren't going to be easy.

Placing her suitcase in the room she'd claimed during the summer she'd spent with Gram when she was eighteen years old, Lottie stripped off her clothes. The en suite bathroom was as uniquely decorated as the rest of the house with its colorful decor. Nothing matched, yet it all blended in a way that somehow fit. Just like Gram.

The tension in her shoulders relaxed beneath the shower's hot water. Gram was going to be fine. Yes, she'd shattered her foot and ankle in multiple places—how had she done that with a simple fall?—but she would heal and be back to combing the islands for "treasure" that she repurposed into artwork. Everything would be fine.

Wet hair brushed back and body wrapped in a towel, quite possibly one she'd used as a teen as her earth child grandmother wasn't one for replacing anything that had remaining life, Lottie headed toward the kitchen, planning to search for something to appease her growling belly. Other than the pretzels on the plane that morning, she hadn't eaten. Gram wasn't much of a cook, but always kept a generous supply of the salted caramel, chocolate and the pecan candies that were her weakness. A weakness Lottie had inherited.

Click.

She hugged the towel tighter. Had that been the front door's lock turning, then opening?

Sweat broke out on Lottie's skin. Someone was in her grandmother's house! Had the hire-car driver who'd driven her from the hospital in Beaufort to Fripp Island returned and jimmied the lock to let himself in? She hadn't gotten a bad vibe, but one never knew.

Too bad she hadn't picked up Maritime, Gram's dog, from her neighbor's. A sixty-pound dog being in the house might have caused the intruder to reconsider.

Trying to quietly retrace her steps down the hallway to her room to dig a can of pepper spray from her purse, Lottie bumped into a metal canister that held a variety of colorful glass bottles Gram had rescued from the sea and poked over a large driftwood piece's roots and branches. Clang! She grabbed at the bottles, loosening her towel, which took immediate precedence. In her efforts to grasp the fabric, she hit Gram's piece again. Metal, wood and glass crashed onto the tile. Clackety-clank-clank! Glass shattered about her feet.

So much for whoever was in the house not knowing she was there.

Intending to make a run for her pepper spray, Lottie took a step. A sharp shard sliced deep into her bare foot. "Ouch!"

She couldn't suppress the excruciated cry or the tears that prickled her eyes.

Ignore the pain. Get to your purse.

She'd barely taken two hobbling steps when the hall light flicked on and a ghost from her past stepped into the hallway.

At Jackie Dunlap's request, Lincoln Thomas stopped by her place to ready the house for what would hopefully only be a few days of sitting empty. Unfortunately, he suspected she'd be away from her beloved Fripp longer than she'd claimed during her call. Then again, Jackie was just stubborn enough that it wouldn't surprise him if she'd found a way home that very evening.

Hearing movement in the hallway, then the loud crashing of Jackie's art piece onto the floor, had him pausing long enough inside the foyer to grab a sea-weathered oar from where Jackie had hung it. It wasn't much of a weapon but would still deliver a good whack. Crime was rare on Fripp, but word of Jackie's hospitalization may have gotten out. Had someone broken into her home with plans to search out easily removed valuables while the house sat unattended?

Oar at the ready, Linc mentally prepared himself for whatever was about to happen. Rounding the corner, he saw the one thing—the one person—he could never fully be prepared to face even though he'd imagined seeing her again hundreds of times over the past twelve years.

"Lottie." Saying her name out loud had his heart hammering even faster. Maybe he'd rounded the corner and he'd been the one hit in the head. His was certainly spinning enough he'd believe something had hit him. Outside of his dreams, he hadn't set eyes on Lottie Fairwell since he'd been nineteen and so in love with her that he'd barely been able to think for how his heart had pounded when near her. His heart was pounding crazy right now.

Lottie!

"Linc!" Green gaze wide, eyeing his still raised weapon, she hugged the towel, which barely covered her midsection.

"What are you doing here?" they asked in unison.

Not that Linc couldn't guess. She'd returned because of her grandmother's fall. Jackie hadn't mentioned Lottie's return when she'd asked him to check her place. Had she known her only grandchild was home? He'd thought it was odd that she hadn't asked her next-door neighbor, who'd taken Jackie's Carolina dog home with her the night before, to ready the house, but he'd agreed to go by as soon as he'd finished sand-ing the bathroom walls he'd spackled earlier that week in his dream house. Well, he was working to transform it into his dream house.

Lottie was on Fripp.

Linc fought to keep his eyes on her face rather than the body that had haunted his dreams for over a decade. Maybe one's first love always set the bar by which to measure all others. Either way, he'd gotten over that nonsense years ago. It was just the adrenaline rush of not knowing who was in the house that had his heart slamming against his rib cage.

But that didn't keep his insides from stirring at the fact that, except for the flimsy towel, Lottie was naked and less than ten feet from him. How was that supposed to not resurrect memories? Her toned body had filled out a little with age but was otherwise just as he recalled. Although a busy cardiologist in Boston, she obviously took time to stay in shape. With her wet blond hair combed back from her makeup-free face, she looked much as she had the summer they'd spent every spare second together. The summer they'd fallen madly in love with one another. Summer love. Teen love. Real and yet, not.

"Linc, I— Am I imagining that you're here?" Shifting her weight, she grimaced, as if in pain, then arched her right foot, its nails painted bubblegum-pink, and balanced on her toes.

"You're cut." Guilt hit that he'd been so

stunned at seeing her that he'd missed what should have been obvious.

Taking in the blood trickling onto the floor, she lifted her gaze back to his. A pleading emotion shone in the green depths of her eyes for the briefest second before they went blank. Her lids closed and, skin losing all color, her body went lax.

"Lottie!"

"You always were one for dramatics, but I never expected you to fall into my arms first thing."

Lottie recognized the voice. It was one she'd never forget. How could she when it belonged to Linc? Her sweet, sweet Linc, with whom she'd spent hours exploring Fripp the summer before she'd left for university.

She hadn't heard his voice outside of her dreams in more than a decade. The events of the past twenty-four hours swirled through her consciousness. Gram had broken her foot and was in the hospital. Lottie had flown to South Carolina and was in Fripp. A noise had startled her. Had she fallen and hit her head and because of where she was, where she'd spent that magical summer prior to her leaving for university and his working a construction job on the island, her brain was filling in that Linc was there?

No, she hadn't fallen. Strong arms wrapped

around her, carried her. Linc's arms. Eyes still closed because they were too heavy to open, she breathed in. Her senses exploded as he filled her nostrils. He smelled the same, all spice, sea and man. With his teasing tone mixed with concern, he sounded the same. He'd always teased her, made her laugh at herself and the world. He felt the same, too. *Better.* His boyish nineteen-year-old body had filled out, his chest thicker, his shoulders broader, his arms stronger. Lottie swallowed the lump forming in her throat. How long had it been since she'd been so aware of a man? Brian certainly didn't elicit such strong responses from her senses. Not that he'd tried in eons. These days they felt more like friends than a couple.

"I'll give you a little slack since that's a nasty cut on your foot," Linc continued. "But I'm positive there's some rule that doctors aren't allowed to pass out at the sight of blood."

Her throbbing foot registered. She'd stepped on broken glass. Heat flooded Lottie's face. She was never opening her eyes. She was practically naked and in Linc Thomas's arms within seconds of seeing him. Some things never changed. It sure hadn't taken him long to have his way with her that summer. Or had it been her who'd had her way with him? The specifics blurred, just that they'd been young, healthy and in love.

That their relationship had been so physical had seemed a natural progression of the sweet nothings they whispered to each other. Linc had been her first and she'd never regretted that, not even after they'd ended things. Or maybe she had wished she'd never known what it felt like to be with Linc so she wouldn't have such high expectations and could possibly move forward with her relationship with Brian without wishing she could describe his kisses as more than just so-so.

"I think I recognize this towel," Linc continued. "It looks like the one we used to take to Pritchard's with us and that the wind caught that time. I had to wade out into the water to retrieve it, remember?"

There had been nothing so-so about the kisses she'd gotten that day. Goose bumps prickled her skin as she recalled lying on a blanket with Linc, the ocean playing a song just for them and their bodies dappled with moonlight. With his fevered kisses and gentle touch, he'd coaxed her body to the ultimate in pleasure. Whispering his affections, he'd promised to love her forever. But by forever, he'd clearly meant only until summer's end.

"Ah, there's some color in those lovely high-boned cheeks of yours." His tone was teasing, as if he knew she was conscious and purposely keeping her eyes closed. Did he also know where her mind had gone? That part of her wanted to beat her fists against his chest that he'd ended things, that when she'd thought she might die from missing him, he'd ignored her heartfelt voice mail declaring her love and desire to come back to him? Saying that she was willing to go to university close to wherever his next construction job took him?

"I was beginning to wonder if you were going to come to on your own," he continued, his arms strong around her, "or if I was going to have to do mouth-to-mouth to wake you."

Face hot, she opened her eyes, looking into the bluest eyes she'd ever seen. Eyes that seemed to look right through to her very soul. She'd once bared all she was to him, which hadn't been difficult since he'd always known what she was thinking, anyway. The way his eyes sparkled had her wondering if he still had that power. Did he know her body had instantly come alive at his nearness? Did he have any idea how many nights she'd cried herself to sleep because he'd said it was better for them to end things rather than try to maintain a long-distance relationship and end up tainting their perfect summer together?

Why didn't you call me back?

"No mouth-to-mouth." She wished she could

bury her face in his chest rather than reveal to him whatever it was he saw in her gaze.

As those all-seeing eyes continued to search hers, one corner of his mouth hiked up. "Too bad."

Seriously? Anger and frustration hit.

"Put me down!" She put a hand protectively over the towel to make sure it didn't slip. Why was he still holding her? Why was he even there?

More and more senses popped to life as the feel of his arms against her bare legs registered, as the once tightly tucked towel now rode up her hips. If there had been anyone else in the room, they'd have gotten an eyeful.

"So that you can bleed on Jackie's floor?" Shaking his head, he set her on the kitchen countertop.

Lottie kept her arms tightly around herself, making sure the towel stayed in place as she crossed her legs to try to decrease how exposed she felt. Why hadn't she wrapped two or three of the things around her? Or better yet, gotten dressed? Then again, she hadn't known she was going to be face-to-face with anyone, much less her past.

Linc examined the bottom of her foot. His blue eyes, fringed with dark lashes, lifted. For the briefest of moments, it struck her that his eyes no longer held the adoration that they had in the past when he'd always gazed upon her with passionate love. Deep loss hit. Ridiculous. It's been over for twelve years. She did not expect Linc to gaze upon her with adoration—but the fact that he wasn't was doing odd things to her that felt akin to grief, as though she'd lost something precious. Bringing up things she'd grieved long ago and gotten over, moved on from.

"You aren't going to like this," he warned, still holding her foot, "but I need to clean off the blood to see if there's glass in there."

Yeah, he was right. She wasn't going to like that. Nor did she like that her brain was more aware of his strong, yet gentle fingers holding her foot than it was of the glass that was definitely still in there.

"I can do it," she insisted, feeling more and more self-conscious. She'd imagined seeing Linc again more times than she could count. They'd bump into each other. He'd see the accomplished cardiologist she'd become, that she'd moved on and had a great life, and he'd realize how wrong he'd been to let her go. Not once in those imaginings had she been soaking wet, wrapped in a towel and bleeding while he looked like hunky male perfection.

"Letting me would be easier."

True, and yet, nothing had ever been further

from the truth. Nothing about Linc was easy. Not the way he held her, not the way his eyes no longer held affection, not the way he sounded so immune to her presence, when she was so off-kilter.

"Turn so that I can rinse off your foot in the sink," he requested. "And hang on to your towel."

No worries there. Lottie clung to the towel for dear life as she scooted to where she could drop her foot into the ceramic basin. Linc flipped on the faucet, then checked to make sure the temp was okay. When satisfied, he took the nozzle, sprayed her foot and gently cleansed away the blood.

Watching him, a hundred emotions hit. This was Linc. The young man who had been her first love. Her first lover. Her first heartbreak. Linc.

"I'm sorry you're having to do this. I really could have." Sitting on the kitchen countertop with her foot in the sink, wearing only a towel, was about as awkward a reunion as she could imagine.

"It's not a big deal." He shrugged as if it truly wasn't. He'd clearly forgotten her long ago, writing off what they'd shared as summer love that had been wonderful, but never meant to last.

His fingernail scraped over the glass, sending a sharp pain all the way up her leg.

"Ow." She jerked free from his grasp.

"Sorry. I didn't mean to hurt you."

But you did. Hating her thoughts, she closed her eyes, counted to ten, then opened them to find that he was watching her.

"You okay?"

No. Yes.

"Fine."

"Good. There for a second I thought you were about to black out again." Reaching into a nearby drawer, he pulled out a dish towel. He gently wrapped the fabric around her foot to prevent blood from dripping, taking care not to put any pressure over the area with the glass so as not to push it deeper. Moving to the cabinet that contained Gram's odds and ends, he rummaged until he found her first aid kit, which had been buried beneath boxes. He removed gauze and alcohol pads. "I need tweezers to get the glass from your foot. It's deep, but I can see it and can hopefully grab hold without having to dig it out. I can't imagine Jackie not having at least one pair in her art supplies. I'm going to go look. I'll disinfect them prior to removing your friend, there."

He obviously wasn't going to leave until he'd extracted the glass.

"There are tweezers in my makeup bag in my bathroom. They're inside a little travel kit."

His brow arched. "Is it okay if I get them?"

Realizing he was asking permission to go into her private bathroom, Lottie nodded. It wasn't as if it made sense to tell him no. She had glass in her foot. He was planning to remove it. No matter how many mind games her head was playing, it was really nothing more than Linc being helpful the same as he'd have done if she was a complete stranger.

When he returned, he didn't comment, just lifted her foot and after a few failed attempts that had Lottie gritting her teeth and clenching her fists, he pulled out a chunk of glass.

"There. Got it." He placed the tweezers and offending blue glass on the countertop, then pressed gauze to the wound. "Hold that while I find an adhesive bandage. There weren't any in the first aid kit."

"Gram's forever nicking her fingers while working on a project and keeps them out. They're—" She paused as he searched the cluttered built-in desk to one side of the kitchen. "You remember where she keeps them."

Opening one of the bandage strips, he placed it across her cut, then applied pressure to the area with his thumb. "I remember a lot of things."

Her heart thudded to a halt, then jerked hard. "I, uh, that's good."

His gaze locked with hers; he lifted his brow. "Is it, Lottie?"

Why did she get the impression he wasn't referring to where her grandmother stored things?

He glanced back at where he held her foot. "You'll be a little sore, but you should be good as new within a few days."

"Thank you."

"I should be thanking you for the glimpse at my past."

Heat flooded her face, and she adjusted the towel, making sure not to uncover her top while trying to fully hide her bottom as she crossed her arms over her chest. "A gentleman wouldn't look."

"I actually meant—" He shook his head, then losing his serious expression, he chuckled. "That wasn't what I meant, but don't sweat your terry cloth fashion statement, Lottie. It's nothing I haven't seen before."

More heat infused her cheeks.

"That was a long time ago." She hadn't expected to see Linc while in Fripp. Not once over the years since her preuniversity summer had their paths crossed. Originally from northern Florida, he'd only been on Fripp for his job. Yet, she never came back without wondering what it would be like to see him again.

Ha, who was she kidding? It didn't take visiting Fripp to make her wonder about Linc.

"Yep. It was." His gaze stayed locked with hers, almost as if he was searching for the girl she'd once been, the one who'd run into his waiting arms and showered him with kisses with complete abandon. Maybe it was that pure happiness she'd felt that summer, her world had been right, carefree, that had made them seem so perfect. So much had changed since then that it was no wonder her psyche clung to that summer as the happiest she'd ever been.

"But, like I said—" Linc's thumb eased its pressure against her foot "—I remember a lot of things."

Linc certainly hadn't forgotten Lottie. Not that he hadn't tried. He had. Especially in the months following when she'd first left South Carolina. Sometimes, he thought he'd gone a little crazy during that time. Maybe he had, especially after her phone call. But she'd been an upper middle class young woman about to leave to start school at Harvard, and he'd been nothing more than a poor kid working a construction job to help put himself through community college. He hadn't needed her mother to point out those stark differences to him.

Memories had his jaw clenching and he fought

sighing. Things had worked out as they should have, though. He and Lottie had both gone on to become the people they were meant to be. Her a cardiologist as she and her parents had wanted. And, although he hadn't known at that time that it was what he wanted for his future, he loved being a physical therapist. Ending things and leaving them ended had been the right thing. But holding Lottie, feeling her skin against his again after so much time, even under such innocent circumstances, was blurring the lines of the present and the past.

"This isn't the first time I've removed something from your foot."

She bit into her lower lip.

"We'd been walking on the beach," he continued, letting the past wash over him, "and you stepped on a shell, crushing it. A piece stuck in your foot."

"I really need to learn to wear shoes, eh?" She stared down at where he held her foot. "You carried me piggyback to Gram's. I could have walked, but you wouldn't let me."

"She wasn't home. You thanked me with a kiss." More than a kiss. Much, much more.

A strangled noise came from deep in her throat. "I wouldn't expect a repeat of that."

Was she remembering how they'd ended up in her room, in that bed that flooded him with memories when he'd gone after her tweezers earlier? He'd made love to her, told her his dreams, felt her cup his face as she told him how being with him was like living a fantasy.

Being on Fripp that summer had been a fantasy. Unfortunately, they'd both had to return to reality. Lottie's reality hadn't included someone like him. Everyone had known that except her.

"No kiss?" Why was he pushing? Teasing her? He didn't want or expect a kiss of gratitude from Lottie, or anything more. "Good thing I wasn't."

Linc refocused on her foot. Lifting his thumb, he was glad to see she hadn't bled through the bandage. "Looks as if you've stopped bleeding. My work here is done." How mundane they sounded. Then again, why wouldn't they? Picking up the used gauze and tape, he tossed them into the trash bin beneath the cabinet.

"How is it that you know where everything is located in Gram's home?" Lottie asked from where she still sat on the counter.

Jackie mentioned Lottie to him from time to time. Did she not do the same with her granddaughter? Telling Lottie that he now lived on Fripp? That she'd invited him over multiple times since he'd become her neighbor and vice versa?

"It's not as if she's rearranged things since we

were teens. Despite being such a creative person, she's also very much a creature of habit."

Studying him, she frowned. "That's true. I guess what I'm really wondering is why are you here, Linc? In my grandmother's house?"

"She asked me to come by to make sure everything was locked and okay for her to be away for a few days." His explanation contorted her face. "It's a bit confusing to me, too, since you're here, which she failed to mention. I'm guessing she didn't give you a heads-up, either?"

Lottie's forehead crinkled. "Gram sent you here? Why would she do that?"

He shrugged. "I assumed it was because she knew I wouldn't mind stopping by since I'd either be home or go by here on my way home."

Her eyes widened. "Home? You live on Fripp?"

She looked incredulous. Did she still think him the poor construction worker he'd been at nineteen? That she'd been the only one to obtain her dreams? Granted, her dreams had stayed on track and his ambitions had changed. But he liked his life and was proud of what he'd achieved, both in construction and as a physical therapist.

"I bought the old McMahon place when it was put up for sale this spring." His bid hadn't been the highest, but the McMahons had accepted anyway as the higher bidders wanted to tear down the house to build a much larger, modern structure and the family hadn't wanted that to happen to their late mother's place.

"I can't believe you live on Fripp in the house I always loved." Still sitting on the countertop with her thighs crossed, she hugged the towel tighter over her chest. "For that matter, I can't believe you're here and that I'm not imagining you."

Leaning against the kitchen island, he eyed her. "Why would you imagine me here, Lottie?"

Had she thought of him over the years? Of course, she had. He'd been her first. If nothing else, that would always set him apart from any lover she'd had since. Fingers curling into his palms, he recognized he had no right to feel the jealousy that punched him at the thought of anyone touching what had once been his.

And to think he'd thought he was going to do a quick walk-through at Jackie's place, then get back to working on his bathroom remodel. Nothing so mundane as that when Lottie Fairwell had returned.

Her lashes lowered, hooding her green eyes. "I, uh, you know."

Pretending a calm he didn't feel, he shook his head. "I don't. Tell me."

Her cheeks pinkened. "No matter. I don't know why I even said that. Just poor word choice.

Anyway, thank you for coming by to check on Gram's house, but there's no need. I'm here."

"For how long?"

"I'm not sure." Concern etched itself onto her lovely features and remorse hit at the circumstances that had triggered her return. "As long as Gram needs me and that I can manage away from work. That's not a problem, is it?"

A thousand problems. More.

"Why would that be a problem? Whether or not you're in Fripp makes no difference to me, Lottie." Only, it did. Knowing Lottie was on Fripp, that she was so close, had every nerve ending in his body short-circuiting. "Since you're here and can keep an eye on things for Jackie, I'll head home."

Indecision shone in her green depths. "I... It was good to see you, Linc. Unexpected, but good."

"Uh, yeah, it was good to see you, too."

"I'd walk you to the door, but I'm afraid of just how much you'd see if I attempt to get down."

Running his gaze over her bare shoulders, arms and legs, realizing that if she slid off the counter, the towel likely would shift to reveal the curve of her thighs, maybe more, Linc swallowed and pushed himself away from the kitchen island. "I'll let myself out. Welcome back to Fripp, Lottie."

"Just temporarily, though," she reminded him.

Yet another thing he hadn't forgotten.

For Lottie, Fripp had never been anything more than an escape from reality.

A wise man would keep that in mind.

CHAPTER TWO

"ANYTHING INTERESTING HAPPEN last night?" Gram asked within seconds of Lottie's arrival at Beaufort Hospital the following morning.

Any doubt that her grandmother hadn't purposely sent Linc dissipated.

"You shouldn't have done that." Keeping her weight mostly off her right foot, Lottie kissed her grandmother's cheek. Although not enough to make her limp, her foot had been sore when she'd cleaned the area and put a fresh adhesive bandage over it that morning.

"Done what?" Gram's eyes, so similar to Lottie's, sparkled as she blinked innocently. As if. Lottie doubted her grandmother had ever been innocent, and that had played a huge role in why Lottie's mother had guarded all interaction she'd had with Gram. Vivien had protested Lottie's decision to spend that summer with her grandmother, but Lottie had longed to know the grandmother she'd only seen a few times.

She narrowed her gaze at the woman she loved with all her heart. "You know exactly what. Shame on you."

"Oh, that." Gram chuckled. "To be fair, I'd planned to ask Linc to go by before you got home."

"In South Carolina, you mean? Not home."

"You always said Fripp felt like home." Gram's brow lifted. "Has that changed?"

Placing her oversize purse next to the more comfortable appearing visitor chair of the two in the room, Lottie sat down. Being cautious so as not to alert Gram of her injury, she angled her foot to where her weight balanced on the back of her heel. "Let's just say that having you in the hospital is messing with my sense of homecoming."

"Yours and mine both." Gram gave her a sly look. "Did Linc tell you that he's my neighbor?"

Trying to appear nonchalant, Lottie pulled out her laptop from her bag. "He mentioned he'd bought the McMahon house. Good for him."

"He's only been there a few months and is restoring the place. Jean had been sick for so long that the house had run down while sitting mostly empty over the past couple of years." Gram's forehead squished with thought. "Before that, she tended to stay in just a few rooms so didn't notice how neglect was affecting the house."

"I recall you mentioning a few years back that she'd moved in with her son. I was sorry to hear that she had died last year. I know you'd been neighbors for decades." Lottie had never been able to decide if the two women were anything more than frenemies as they continually bickered and were rivals at everything they did, but Gram had been truly saddened when she told Lottie the news.

"Our card club hasn't been the same since she got sick. She and Gerty were the only ones who could beat me and Mary. Who would have thought that winning all the time would be so boring?" Gram rearranged the white top sheet covering her. "I was glad when her family sold her place to Linc. Apparently, he'd been looking for a while and his real estate agent contacted him the moment it went on the market."

His purchase hadn't been a random, spur of the moment impulse, but something he'd thought out. Duh, it's a house. An expensive house. Of course, he'd had to plan for its purchase.

At her grandmother's expectant look, she said, "It's always been a beautiful place."

"But in need of a lot of TLC, which Linc's giving the ole girl. Although he hired contractor friends to help with the outside, he's doing most of the work himself. It's looking great. He's a very talented young man."

Gram had no idea.

Lottie fought to keep her cheeks from heating. No way would her grandmother miss that telltale sign that Lottie was affected by her ramblings about Linc. Why had Gram not mentioned him a single time? She must have been busting on the inside knowing she was setting Lottie up to come face-to-face with him. Unlike Lottie's mother, Gram had adored Linc.

"I like your new piece, Gram. Is it commissioned or will it be going to the gallery in Charleston?"

Her grandmother's expression said she knew Lottie had purposely changed the subject away from Linc, but she acquiesced. Probably because Lottie had changed it to her art. Gram's true passion was her artwork, and few things took precedence over that.

"It's just something I've been working on, but maybe I will send it to Charleston. They've been asking me to get them more pieces." Gesturing to where she lay in the bed, she frowned. "I really don't have time for being laid up like this. Terrible timing."

"Is there ever a good time for fractures, Gram?" Lottie's question earned a scowl, but before Gram spouted a comeback, someone knocked on the hospital room door. Both women glanced that way. Carrying a beautiful flower arrangement, Linc walked into the room. All the oxygen took a hiatus, leaving Lottie light-headed. She hadn't imagined how hunky grown-up Linc was. The man was hot.

He smiled at Gram. "Good morning, Jackie."

What he wore registered. Navy scrubs that fit just right everywhere except his biceps. There they appeared not too tight for comfort, but a little snug. He'd always had a body well-honed from work. Those arms and how easily he'd scooped her up the night before attested that hadn't changed. Lottie bit into her lower lip. Her gaze dropped to his ID badge. Lincoln Thomas, PT, DPT. He'd gone to physical therapy school and gotten a doctorate degree? When had he de-cided to pursue patient care? Then again, had she expected him to be the same person now that he'd been back then? Of course, he'd grown, changed, just as she had. Recalling how gentle he'd been with her foot, she admitted she could see him working with patients and being very good at what he did. Still, the different career path he'd taken was a shocker.

Eyeing the flowers he held, her grandmother's face lit. "Linc! We were just talking about you. Are those flowers for my beautiful granddaugh-ter? They're gorgeous." Lottie's face caught fire. "The blue moons, chicories, cornflowers and phlox mixed in with spartina grass and dried palm fronds in that shell-covered vase makes me think of the sea."

Linc just grinned and placed the flowers on the tray table. "You know you're my best girl, Jackie. I thought you'd like the colors."

Gram beamed. "It's like having a bit of the island here with me."

"I'm impressed. It's the perfect arrangement for Gram."

"I thought so. How's your foot?"

"Fine," Lottie and her grandmother answered at the same time. Lottie grimaced.

Gram frowned. "What happened to your foot?"

Lottie wrinkled her nose at Linc. "You just had to tell on me, didn't you?"

Not looking the slightest repentant, he shrugged. "I figured you had already told her all the drama she caused. You didn't think you could replace those bottles and her not know the difference?"

"What bottles?" Gram's gaze bounced back and forth between them. "What happened that's my fault?"

"I knocked your bottles off the large hallway piece." She narrowed her gaze at her grandmother. "For the record, I refuse to take blame for the break as, had you mentioned that you'd asked Linc to stop by, I wouldn't have been frightened to hear someone."

A tiny bit of remorse flickered. "I'm sorry that you were frightened. Now, what happened to your foot?"

"I cut my foot on a glass shard. Linc got the glass out." Wondering at her giddiness that he was near, she glanced his way. "Thanks again."

"You're welcome. Sore?"

"A little. It only hurts when I step down. Thanks for asking." Listen to them sounding all polite with Gram as their avid audience. The surface might be mundane politeness, but peel away that layer and kinetic energy threatened to burst free. She didn't like the Richter-scale worthy rumbling in her chest, though. It was completely normal to feel shaky when one reconnected with their first love, right?

"No problem." Had his voice sounded a little shaky, too? Or had Lottie imagined that? Either way, he turned toward Gram. "I hear you're going to surgery in the morning."

"Gram!" Lottie frowned. "You didn't tell me you were scheduled for surgery."

"You didn't ask," she said matter-of-factly, as if Lottie should have known to do so. "Nor had I a chance to tell you, not with us talking about how excited you were to see Linc last night."

Heaven help her.

"You were excited to see me?" Amusement

laced his words to where she knew he was well aware of what Gram was doing.

"That's not what we were talking about." She avoided looking toward him for fear her eyes might reveal that she had been excited and that his teasing tone pinged a whole lot of feel-good memories. "Um—" she cleared her throat "—Gram, tell me what the surgeon said."

Gram was still looking back and forth between Lottie and Linc. "He's going to pin me back together like one of my pieces of art. He's worried that with my heel having multiple fractures that if he doesn't pin it together like some type of jigsaw puzzle that it'll refracture when I put weight on it. It's not going to be able to bear weight for at least four weeks, maybe longer. Four weeks of no walking, maybe not even with crutches." She frowned. "What would using crutches hurt?"

"He's afraid that you'd end up putting weight on your foot by accident," Linc suggested from where he stood next to Gram's bed. He spoke to Gram, but Lottie could feel his gaze still on *her*. "He doesn't want your recovery to have a setback."

Gram patted his hand. "Enough about my surgery. Let's talk about my house. Everything looked good when you stopped by last night?"

"Yeah, everything looked just as I remembered."

Why did Lottie think he wasn't talking about the house?

"There was no need for Linc to come by last night, Gram." There. She sounded halfway composed.

Her grandmother wore a "duh" expression. "Of course, there was. Much better for you and Linc to bump into each other for the first time in the privacy of my house rather than here. Don't you agree, Linc?"

Lottie hadn't thought of it that way, but Gram had a point.

"Well?" Gram asked.

Lottie met Linc's gaze, and he chuckled. "Don't look at me. She's your grandmother. I'm just a neighbor."

"And a good one," Gram said. "You'll keep an eye on Ole Bessie? Stop by and make sure Lottie's okay?"

Lottie shook her head. "I'm thirty years old and haven't needed anyone to stop by to check on me in years."

"Maybe not, but I'll rest better knowing Linc's keeping an eye on you and my house." Gram's shoulders sagged, and a rather pitiful look come over her face.

Linc smiled at Jackie's nickname for her

house, Ole Bessie, named after a beloved child-hood dog.

"No worries, Jackie. You just focus on getting well. I'll keep an eye on your place and on Lottie while you're away. Anything in particular you want me to watch for?"

Delighted by his response, Gram's eyes sparkled. "Just make sure my two girls are taken care of."

The following morning, Gram wasn't nearly as perky as the day before, and she told Lottie her surgery had been postponed. During the night, her blood pressure had dropped, and her nurse had had to call Dr. Collins. They'd made medication tweaks. Although still a little lower than her baseline, her pressure had improved. Thank goodness.

Dr. Collins checked on Gram, but she was still pale and irritable.

"I'm not taking you into surgery this afternoon, but I'm ordering more labs." Empathy showed on Dr. Collins's face. "If you behave, we'll get you in the operating room in the morning to put your foot back together."

Jackie gave him an unhappy, squinty-eyed look. "Isn't that what you said yesterday?"

He held her gaze. "If you want out of this

place, then don't give the nurse a reason to wake me up during the night, again."

Her grandmother didn't seem amused. "Fine. Surgery tomorrow, then home. But you'd better not change your mind again."

"Don't give me a reason to."

Gram mumbled something under her breath.

After Dr. Collins had left the room, Gram sighed. "He's just delaying my surgery for kicks."

"I'm sure that's his reason," Lottie agreed, causing Gram to cut her gaze toward her.

"Aren't you full of sass today?"

Lottie leaned over and kissed her grandmother's cheek. "I can't help myself. It's my genetics."

Whether the kiss or the comment, Gram grinned and relaxed against her pillow. "That it is. Lucky girl. How's my house?"

"I haven't torn it down yet."

Gram frowned. "Bite your tongue. How about my baby?"

"Maritime is fine." She'd picked up the blasted dog from the neighbor's the night before and dropped him off that morning. "The house is fine, Gram. They're both waiting on you to come home when you're back on your feet."

Gram's gaze narrowed. "Did Linc come by?"

"The house?" Lottie shook her head. "Not

since when you forgot to let him know I was home. Why would he come by?"

"You know why he'd come by. To check on you like I asked him."

"I know you're matchmaking, Gram, but don't, okay? You know I'm in a relationship with Brian." Things were complicated enough without her grandmother's interference. Lottie took a deep breath. "You always did like Linc."

"So did you."

"Yes," she agreed, knowing there was no reason to deny it. She'd liked him right up until they'd said their goodbyes and he'd meant his. "He was a great guy."

"He still is," Gram mused, looking thoughtful. "Your first love."

"But not my grown-up love," Lottie reminded her. A vision of her mother telling her those very words flashed through her mind. She'd been miserable with missing Linc, had confessed to her mother that she was transferring to a medical school in South Carolina. Vivien had been aghast at the thought, telling her she was not throwing her future away on a silly summer love.

Linc had been a summer love, her first love, her first everything. No doubt that was why she felt so connected to him, why seeing him again had her so off-kilter. If he'd answered her call

all those years ago, would she have been able to win him back? To convince him that what they'd had was more than a summer fling? Or would she have been making the biggest mistake of her life by throwing away all of her other dreams to chase after her heart's desire?

If he'd really loved her, he'd have returned her call. He hadn't. Her mother had been right to beg her not to throw her life away on a man who expected her to make all the concessions.

Lottie had loved Linc so much that she'd have dug ditches if it meant being with him, but she'd never meant that much to him. She'd thought she had, but she'd been so naive…

"If thinking about that doctor guy puts that look on your face," Gram said, interrupting her thoughts, "then I was wrong about him."

Guilt hit and Lottie fought hard to keep it from showing. "I'm both shocked that you admitted you were wrong and curious as to exactly what you're wrong about."

"I never believed you loved the doctor. When I'm wrong, I admit it." Gram fluffed her pillow, then settled back against it. "I promise to be nicer if our paths cross again."

Lottie's gaze shifted to her grandmother's. "That would be good. Brian doesn't think you like him."

Gram shrugged. "I don't dislike him."

"He's a good man." Everyone told her how lucky she was that they were a couple. Her roommate, Camilla, went on and on about how crazy Lottie was to have not already married him. Lottie's mother had wanted nothing more than for Brian to be her son-in-law. "You'd like Brian if you gave him a chance."

Gram shook her head. "Doubtful. He convinced you to stay in Boston rather than practice in South Carolina. You do realize that just because your mother approved of him doesn't mean you have to stay with him, don't you? Staying with him won't bring her back."

Lottie's throat tightened at Gram's blunt words. "Mom isn't why I'm with Brian, Gram. Nor is he why I stayed in Boston. I had an amazing job offer at the hospital to be a part of a great team that's making a difference to so many cardiac patients. Brian is only part of my life in Boston."

A small part, she realized. When not working, she had her friends and usually when she and Brian were together, it was as part of group events or with Camilla. Maybe that's why he felt more like a friend than her significant other these days. It had been eons since they'd spent any quality time together as a couple, and she couldn't recall the last time they'd done more than a quick kiss goodbye or hello.

Why had Brian's kisses never set her on fire the way a nineteen-year-old young man's had?

"I said I was wrong too soon," Gram said, interrupting her thoughts again. "Your normal look when we discuss the doctor is back."

Curiosity got the better of Lottie. "What look is that?"

"Resignation."

"Here. I thought you could use this."

Leaning back in the chair she occupied in the operating room waiting area, Lottie glanced up to see Linc holding out a coffee cup. A wooden stir stick stuck up through the lid. Today, he wore perfectly fitting black scrubs and his hospital ID badge. His hair looked a little ruffled, as if he'd run his fingers through the sun-kissed brown locks a few times.

Every time Gram's door had opened the day before, Lottie's heart had done an anticipatory quiver that had been followed by disappointment when it hadn't been Linc. He hadn't come by but had called Gram to tell her he wasn't working and had previous plans with a couple of friends helping him hang Sheetrock so wouldn't be making the drive to Beaufort for a visit.

"Thanks." She took the coffee before her fingers reached up to see if his hair was as soft as her memory believed. Twelve years, and yet if she closed her eyes, she could see everything from that long-ago summer, could hear the sounds, smell the scents. Probably because the memory of him had never been far from her consciousness.

Popping the lid, she lifted the cup to breathe in the strong brew's aroma. Her stomach growled in appreciation. She'd been too nervous to eat. Maybe she still was, but having the coffee in hand provided a momentary distraction from the fact that Gram was in surgery and Linc had just sat down in the chair opposite from hers.

"Want these?" Reaching into his scrubs pocket, he pulled out a single sugar and creamer. Just how she liked her coffee.

Taking his offering, she eyed him. "Is it a coincidence that you brought one sugar and one creamer, or did you remember that's how I liked my coffee?"

"Coincidence."

Lottie didn't believe him. Then again, with the grin on his face, had he meant for her to?

He watched her tear open the sugar packet. "Any word yet?"

Pouring the contents into her cup, she shook her head. "I was hoping that's why you were here, to give me an update."

"Sorry. I've been with patients all morning. Other than swinging by the cafeteria to grab your coffee, I came straight here from the therapy room."

She lifted the cup to take a tentative sip of the hot liquid, realized she hadn't put in her creamer, and wasn't sure if it was his being there or nervousness over waiting to hear about Gram's surgery that had her so discombobulated. "Gram's surgeon didn't foresee any complications, but this waiting is killing me."

The only other time she'd been in a waiting area in a nondoctor role had been when she'd gotten the call about her parents' wreck. That hadn't ended well. No wonder she was a bundle of nerves.

"Gram's going to be okay." Was she talking to Linc or reassuring herself? "It's just surgery to repair her foot."

"Waiting is never easy, but especially not when you're used to being on the other side of medicine." Linc's gaze held kindness, as if he knew, and yet, he couldn't. Although he'd caused the first, he hadn't been there either time her heart had broken.

Knowing she had to get her thoughts away from the past before it pulled her down a hole she rarely let herself fall into, she took a deep breath. "You're right. I'm usually the one delivering news of how a procedure went, rather than being the concerned family member. Maybe that's why I feel as if I should be doing something rather than just sitting here waiting and waiting and waiting."

One corner of Linc's mouth lifted. "Patience was never one of your virtues."

Pouring in the creamer, she stirred the steaming mixture. "I was eighteen when you knew me. How many eighteen-year-olds are patient?"

"Good point." He chuckled softly. "Back then we were ready to tackle the world."

"Or at least a whole lot of school." She took another appreciative sip of the coffee. A small sip because the refreshing brew scalded her tongue a little. "Speaking of which, how did you end up in physical therapy? I had thought you were going into construction and planning to start your own company."

Watching as she blew on the coffee to try to cool it, he shrugged. "I thought that, too. When I went back to school that fall, I continued with my business classes and worked construction part-time. I enjoy building, still do, but I realized I wanted to do something more directly hands-on to help people. A coworker got hurt and was with a therapist when I visited. I remember thinking how amazing it must feel to help someone rediscover the things most of us take for granted, such as walking or being able to reach into the kitchen cabinet. I was hooked and knew therapy was what I was meant to do."

His passion for his job came through. He'd once talked just as passionately about someday owning his own construction company and building affordable housing complexes in big cities. Over the years she'd imagined him on construction crews, sometimes as the manager, sometimes being the laborer swinging a hammer. He'd changed his mind about her. Why hadn't she ever considered that he might have changed his mind about his career, too?

Biting into her lip, her gaze lowered to his ID badge. "You work exclusively for the hospital?"

He nodded. "Since moving back to the area, I'm here three days a week. More when covering for someone. I've no complaints. The pay is good, decent benefits and I'm part of a great team."

"What do you do the other four days?" Heat warmed her cheeks. "Sorry. I'm being nosy, aren't I? What you do on your own time is none of my business. Forget I asked."

He shrugged. "It's not a problem. Currently, I'm working on my house and enjoying life."

Lottie worked five, six and sometimes seven days a week. Week after week. She could cut back, she supposed, but there was always so much to be done that rearranging her schedule seemed impossible. Even now, guilt plagued her that Brian and her colleagues were having to cover her patients. When he'd called the night before, they'd talked for less than a minute, with Brian stating he had to go as he was still at the hospital but had wanted to say hi before it got any later. Or maybe it had been because Maritime had gone nuts with her barking when the phone had rung.

Whether she wanted to or not, she couldn't keep from comparing the two men. Handsome and always impeccably put together, Brian had dark hair, dark eyes, and pale skin that rarely saw the light of day. Linc was a relaxed blue-eyed hunk who loved being outdoors. Looking at him, Lottie couldn't help but wonder if it had been more than wanting to finish her residency and focusing on her career that had held her back from agreeing to marry Brian.

"Is there anyone special in your life?" The question had popped into Lottie's head several times since he'd startled her at Gram's. He didn't wear a wedding band and Gram must think he was single, but was he involved? Her stomach twisted. Why did the thought of there being someone special in his life make her belly hurt?

"You don't have to answer if you don't want to," she added, swallowing the knot forming in her throat. "That was me being nosy about something that's none of my business. I can't seem to help myself."

"It's okay. Ask whatever you want, Lottie. We're old friends catching up, so it's not a big deal, right?"

She supposed that was one way of looking at it, but he didn't answer her question. Did that mean there was someone special? What was she thinking? There was someone special in her life. Someone her parents had wanted her to some-day marry. No other man could ever hold that honor. The one in front of her held the distinction of being the one person her mother had begged her to forget.

"To answer your question, there hasn't been anyone special for a while." His gaze bore into hers. "How about you? Is there someone in Boston waiting on you to come home?"

Was Brian waiting on her to come home? Maybe. More likely that, outside of work, he hadn't missed her since they typically only saw each other on the weekends. They worked out of the same clinic, the same hospital, but most days they stayed so busy that their paths didn't cross. How sad was that?

"I'm dating someone." Now why had she been so vague with her answer?

"Is it serious?" Maybe he'd picked up on her hesitancy.

"He's asked me to pick out an engagement ring." Several times, but not lately, she realized, trying to recall just how long it had been since Brian had last hinted that they make it official, and unable to pinpoint when it had been. Was it wrong that she hadn't noticed that he hadn't mentioned getting married in months?

"Serious enough." Linc was quiet a moment. "Is he good to you?"

Good to her? What did he even mean by that? Brian was a thoughtful person, a hard worker and a loyal friend. They understood each other's long work hours and dedication to their patients. Her parents had adored him.

"Yes. He's good to me. He's covering my patients while I'm here. He was very gracious to tell me to not worry, that he'd make sure everyone was taken care of at the clinic."

He's a real find, Lottie. He's going to make you such a great husband.

"He's a cardiologist, too, then?"

Blinking to clear her mother's voice, she nodded. "We have a lot in common."

"That's nice." Linc didn't really sound impressed, more as if he was just acknowledging her comment.

"We met at school, were in a study group together for a class, and became fast friends and study partners. With as much time as we spent together, I suppose it was natural that we became a couple."

They never fought, never disagreed or argued other than about Gram and on that they had agreed to disagree. Their relationship was easy, rather than one of hot emotion. She glanced toward Linc, her gaze connecting with his, and more guilt hit. *That's not just guilt hitting you*, a voice deep within corrected. *That's the hot emotion that has always flooded you when you're near Linc.*

Because he was my first love.

Your first love imprinted itself on you like no other.

"I know it's been a few years, but I'm sorry about your parents."

Lottie's heart squeezed. "Me, too. I can't believe I lost them both in the same instant, but they loved each other so much that I don't think one would have wanted to survive without the other."

"That's a deep love."

"They definitely loved each other." Her mother had been the yin to her father's yang. "I always wanted a love like theirs. It's what they wanted for me, too. Mom loved Brian so much and wanted to plan our wedding someday. I hate that she'll never be able to."

"I'm sure they did." Linc's voice sounded a

little hoarse and he cleared it prior to adding, "Your mother certainly never felt that way about me."

Lottie's breath caught. Heat burned her cheeks. Adrenaline drove her heartbeat faster and faster. Why had she said what she had? What was wrong with her? "Mom only met you that weekend she and Dad came to visit, Linc. She didn't know you. If she had, she'd have liked you, too."

He shrugged as if it didn't matter. "It's water under the bridge."

But there was such an odd look on his face.

Lottie remembered introducing him to her parents, and and they hadn't hidden their looks of disapproval. Her heart ached. She'd known their dismissal of him as not being important had bothered Linc, and she had done her best to reassure him. In the end, it hadn't mattered, but other than when it came to her mother's relationship with Gram, it was the only time she hadn't understood her parents' behavior.

"Linc, I'm sorry about how they treated you that weekend. They were just being overprotective parents, but I know they bordered on rude." Her mother had even acknowledged that once, apologizing, but reminding Lottie how much better off she was with wonderful Brian. Feeling her mother had needed reassurance, Lottie had nodded. With as much as Linc's rejection had hurt, maybe Lottie had even believed it.

"Like I said, water under the bridge." Linc glanced toward his watch. "My next patient arrives soon. Got to get back to the therapy room. Shoot me a text when you hear something about Jackie."

Had he really needed to leave? Or did he just not want to discuss her mother and the past? Who could blame him when he was right; it was water under the bridge.

"Okay." But even as she said it nausea hit. Had he forgotten that after her tearful, almost desperate call, he'd made sure she couldn't reach out again? "I don't have your current number."

When she hadn't heard from him after leaving her miserable voice mail, she'd tried calling again. The number had been disconnected. She'd double-checked that she hadn't dialed the wrong number a few times before admitting the truth to herself.

Linc's left eye twitched ever so slightly, clueing her in that he wasn't as calm as he sounded when he gestured to her phone and asked, "May I?"

She handed the device to him.

He punched in a number, hit dial, then disconnected the call. "Now you have my number and I have yours."

"Just like old times," she said without thought.

"Not even close."

Realizing what he meant, Lottie winced and tried to clarify. "I meant, not like old times as in you and me old times, but…" Shaking her head, she swallowed and started over. "You know what I meant. Go. Your patient will be waiting on you. I'll let you know when I hear something about Gram. Maybe you'll answer this time." Oh, that had been an ugly dig and beneath her. He'd said his goodbye, that it was better for them to end, and he'd stuck to that. Just because she hadn't believed him, had thought he'd come after her to Boston and they'd find a way to make their relationship work, he hadn't done anything wrong.

Linc's face blanched, but he remained silent, just staring down at her as if trying to read beyond her words.

Uncomfortable beneath his stare, she rushed on. "Hopefully I'll hear something soon because I'm worried that Gram's surgery is taking so long. But other than that, you won't hear from me." She tilted her chin upward in a show of bravado she didn't really feel. "Nothing. Not even a peep."

Rather than leave, he stood there, studying her, then raked his fingers through his hair, leaving a fresh rumbled wake. After a moment, his tension eased and he half smiled.

"Not even a peep, eh?" Storms clouded the blue of his eyes, then he stunned her by kissing the top of her head. "Ah, that's more like old times, wouldn't you say?"

Watching as he left the waiting room, Lottie reached up to touch where his lips had lightly grazed her hair.

Her heart pounding as she tried to decipher what had just happened, she whispered, "Not even close."

CHAPTER THREE

"RAISE YOUR LEG a little higher, Jerry. I know you can do it." Linc observed the seventy-year-old huff out a long breath and instead of raising his leg higher, drop it flat against the mat table he lay upon.

"Tell me again how raising my leg is going to make my knee get better."

"It's to strengthen the muscles around your knee so that it stabilizes the joint. Now, get back to work." He'd explained previously, but Jerry, although good-natured, tended to ask the same questions over and over. Linc understood. He'd been doing the same thing, asking himself over and over what he'd been thinking with his foolish kiss to Lottie's head. What had he been thinking? That was it. He hadn't been thinking. So much vulnerability and emotion had shown in her eyes when she'd referred to that unanswered call, that unlike twelve years prior, he'd acted on instinct. "Stupid. Stupid. Stupid."

"Fine. I'm working, but you don't have to call me names," Jerry grumbled, lifting his leg. "I seem to recall you mentioning something about stabilizing the joint."

Linc needed to stabilize his brain. Was there an exercise he could do for that?

"Sorry, Jerry. I was thinking about something I did earlier that I shouldn't have done." Which was all he was going to say out loud on the matter. "Now give me twenty with your toes pointed and twenty with your toes pulled in toward you."

Rather than continue with his leg raises, Jerry's gaze went to something behind Linc. Or more like, someone.

"Ah, now I understand." His patient grinned. "She's pretty."

Even before Linc turned, he knew who Jerry looked at. Only one person had ever made his pulse jump that way. Steeling himself for whatever Lottie had come to say about his idiotic kiss, he faced her. Rather than lambaste him, she tucked her hands into the pockets of her flowy red pants and, a thousand questions in her big green eyes, said, "Sorry. I didn't mean to interrupt. I thought you must be finished with your patient when the receptionist told me to come on in."

"Interrupt. Please interrupt," Jerry pleaded,

earning a glare from Linc. "Fine. Ten pointy toes and ten pulled in toes. Got it."

"It's twenty, not ten," Linc corrected Jerry to give himself a moment. "Besides, rumor has it you missed me when you had your therapy on my day off work."

"You're old enough to know better than to believe rumors," Jerry said, but the man's grin took the edge off his words.

"You'd think I was," Linc agreed. You'd also think him old enough to know better than to have kissed a woman who'd shredded his heart more than a decade ago. Sure, he'd been the one to not call back, but he'd done so for both their sakes. He hadn't needed her mother's interference to know that he'd never be good enough for her precious daughter. He hadn't even blamed Lottie's mother for begging him to stay away and let her daughter have a better life than he'd ever be able to give. Weren't Vivien's words part of what had driven him past every failure and humbled him at each success over the past twelve years?

First making sure Jerry's form was correct, Linc then glanced toward the woman who had turned his insides out the past few days by simply being on Fripp. "Jackie's out of surgery?"

What had Lottie thought about his kiss? It was only a peck to the top of her head, he berated himself. A peck that had him off-kilter. Had it done the same to her? Was that why she'd come in person?

Eyeing him, she nodded. "Again, sorry if I shouldn't be here. I was tired of sitting so after Dr. Collins let me know about Gram, I thought I'd stretch my legs by walking down here to tell you."

Was she wrong to come here? Her eyes seemed to ask. She shifted her weight, first making him wonder if her foot was bothering her, but as she hadn't taken the weight off her right foot, he didn't think so. Instead, he thought she was nervous. Because of him. What did that mean?

"You could have just peeped."

Pink stained her cheeks and he realized that's why she was there. Stubborn, proud, beautiful girl hadn't wanted to call or text. Not even a peep, she'd said.

Oh, Lottie.

He probably needed to stay away from her completely. That would be best. And yet, he knew he wouldn't.

"You think?" she asked, her weight shifting again.

"Stretching your legs is good, too." His imagination immediately jumped to stretching her legs and that was somewhere he definitely needed to keep his mind, and hands, from. To get his brain back on track, he nudged his patient. "See, Jerry, some people intentionally stretch. You should take note."

Jerry rolled his eyes but kept raising his leg. Not as high as Linc would like, so he placed his hand beneath Jerry's ankle and lifted it an inch higher. "Like this."

"Yeah, yeah," Jerry mumbled, but didn't show any signs of discomfort at the increased range of motion. "Just so long as you keep your hands off her, she'll be fine."

Lottie's cheeks went hot pink. Jerry's comment was innocent, but Lottie looked as if she might bolt.

Linc cleared his throat. "You do realize, Jerry, that I'm going to up the ante another inch because you're embarrassing my friend?"

The older man laughed, then gave Lottie a repentant glance. "Sorry. This guy's torture session is affecting my mind. Despite how I'm convinced he enjoys making me hurt, he's a great person. The best. You're lucky to be his girl."

Lottie's mouth opened as she obviously sought a way to tell Jerry that she wasn't his girl. But she had been. For one glorious summer, Lottie had been all his. And he'd willingly let her go.

Even knowing how he hadn't been able to

forget her, he'd do the same thing again. Doing the right thing wasn't always easy or pain free.

"I, uh—" she began, but paused.

Knowing he needed to rescue her and the situation, Linc sighed with great exaggeration. "Now you've really embarrassed her, and me, too, Jerry. She's just a friend."

Just a friend. Linc supposed they were friends. She'd wanted the long-distance relationship when she left for school, but with distance, life circumstances and her mother against them, time would have changed her mind. He'd stayed behind, working and living in a different world from her upper middle class one.

But she was back and thanks to some wise real estate investments, there was no longer an economic disparity between them. Not that Lottie had ever seemed to mind their different backgrounds. Vivien Fairwell had, though. His stomach knotted at the memory of Lottie's mother and her distain that Lottie cared so much for him and how she worried he was going to ruin her baby girl's future.

"Just friends? You should do something about that." Jerry raised up onto his elbows to waggle his brows. "She's much too pretty to be just a friend."

She was pretty. Beautiful. But it had always been more about the sparkle in her eyes and the pull she had on his heart than anything reflected in Lottie's mirror. She had an elusive something that held a power over him that no woman had ever been able to replicate.

"She's only visiting South Carolina because of her grandmother, who happens to be my neighbor, and is in surgery this morning. Lottie came to let me know how Jackie is. Plus she's in a long-term relationship back in Boston."

Had he pointed out the latter as a reminder to himself or for Jerry's sake?

Scratching his balding head, Jerry glanced at Lottie's bare left hand. "I may be missing something but looks as if you've still got a chance. Don't waste it."

Lottie had said the man wanted her to pick out an engagement ring, but she wasn't wearing one. Did that mean she'd declined and that if he wanted to risk it, he had a second chance with her? Loving Lottie had messed with his head and heart for years. Did he want to risk repeating that devastation when she left to go back to Boston?

Because she would go back. It would be foolish to think otherwise.

Whether Lottie was wearing a ring or not didn't matter. Only, he knew that wasn't true. Everything about Lottie mattered. Always had.

Wishing he could see beyond her lovely face

to know what was going on in her mind, Linc met her gaze. "Just as soon as you walk away, I'm unleashing an Intense Pain 101 therapy session. Ignore his screams for mercy and my heinous laughter as I grant him none."

As he'd hoped, Lottie smiled. "Ah, Linc, you should go easy on him. Really, there's no need for the Intense Pain 101 lesson." Her tone was light. "For the record, Linc and I have known each other since we were teenagers, I know what a great guy he is."

Little more than kids? Was that how she saw the people they'd been that summer? Kids who hadn't known better than to love so freely? What would happen if they were just now meeting for the first time, if he didn't know she'd be going back to Boston and her life there? If they didn't have a past that overshadowed the present?

"Just as I know what a great woman she is."

Lottie's breath caught at Linc's compliment. Her gaze connected to his, and his smile dug deep dimples into the corners of his mouth. Even confused as she was, Lottie smiled back. Smiling around Linc came easily. It always had. It was the not being around him that came later that held such heartache and tears.

She never should have come to the therapy room. She'd just been so excited that Gram had come through surgery and done great that she'd needed to tell someone who understood and cared about her grandmother, too. She'd needed to tell Linc.

As it had done often since her arrival, Jerry's gaze bounced between them.

Deciding to make light, she waved her thumb toward Linc. "Jerry, if this guy keeps giving you a hard time, we'll have to rustle up an Intense Pain 101 session for him, instead."

Raising his leg, toe out, Jerry laughed. "You think so?"

Linc's eyes glittered like sunshine bouncing off the sea on the clearest blue day. "You want to make me hurt, Lottie?"

"Maybe," she said with a bright tone and waggle of her brows at Jerry, causing the clueless man to chuckle again. But she faked the lightness, because Linc's question was a valid one. His not wanting to continue their relationship and subsequent ignoring her call had hurt so badly. She'd often thought of someday making him eat his heart out at what he'd rejected. Was that the same thing as wanting him to hurt?

Linc knew. Knew what she was thinking. His smile was still in place, but his gaze had grown intense.

"Everything okay, Linc? Do you need me to finish with Jerry?" A pretty brunette joined them, giving Lottie a look that left no doubt that her interest in Linc went way beyond being his coworker.

Linc hesitated, as if he were considering accepting her offer, which had the woman's smile faltering. She'd obviously expected him to use her interruption as a way of telling Lottie that she needed to leave. Jerry was doing his leg lifts, but Lottie did need to get out of the way.

"Hi, I'm Lottie, an old friend of Linc's." She stuck out her hand toward the woman. "I'm in South Carolina for a week or so while my grandmother recovers from a fall. She lives near Linc. It's nice to meet one of his coworkers."

Was the woman more? The look she was giving said she was trying to decipher the same thing about Lottie. A myriad of emotions hit, jealousy taking up a huge chunk of the pie. Jealousy Lottie had no right to feel.

"Oh, um, that's… Hi." First giving Linc a questioning look, the brunette shook Lottie's hand. "Shannon Simpson, I'm a physical therapist."

"Awesome." Lottie put on her brightest smile, then met Linc's gaze, wishing she could read what was going on behind those guarded blue eyes. Confusion, she guessed. The same as confusion was overwhelming her. "I've got to get to my grandmother's room. Hopefully, she'll be out of recovery and back to herself soon." With that, she smiled at Jerry, then the pretty therapist. "Nice to meet you, Jerry and Shannon. Y'all keep Linc in line."

Y'all? Since when did she say y'all? Since being back in the South, apparently.

Shifting her focus back to the man whose gaze hadn't left her, she waved. "Goodbye, Linc."

The words seemed to echo around the room, bouncing back to smack her with the past and ringing with a finality that went beyond a casual visit. If only she meant it.

"I'll stop by to check on Jackie before I leave this evening," he told her. The way he looked at her suggested he'd like to say something more, but, with their audience, wouldn't.

"Gram will like that." And so would Lottie because he confused her. How nice he was to her, how he'd kissed the top of her head, how there was something deeper when he looked at her that she wished she could fully understand.

"She's one of my favorite people in the world."

"Mine, too. Thanks." Lottie turned to leave, but almost immediately paused at the panicked voice of the woman Shannon had been working with prior to asking Linc if he needed help.

"Shannon? Come quick. Something's wrong."

Shannon, Linc, Jerry and Lottie all looked toward where she had stopped pedaling on the stationary bicycle and was holding her chest. The woman was in her late sixties or perhaps early seventies. Her face was pale. Sweat glistened on her skin surface and dampened the hair along her scalp. Genuine fear showed on her face.

"Mrs. Stephenson?" Shannon crossed the fifteen feet to where her patient tightly gripped the therapy bike's handlebars. "Are you okay?"

Linc and Lottie joined Shannon.

"I… No, my chest is hurting." Grimacing, the woman rubbed her sternum. "It's getting worse."

"Let's get you off the bike," Linc suggested, putting his arm around Shannon's patient to steady her.

Not that Linc needed her help, but Lottie automatically got on the opposite side to assist. He'd obviously meant to guide her to an empty mat table, but Mrs. Stephenson motioned that she wanted to sit immediately so he lowered her to the floor and knelt beside her. "Are you having indigestion? Heartburn?"

Taking a deep breath, then wincing, Mrs. Stephenson shook her head.

Kneeling on the opposite side from Linc, Lottie introduced herself. "Hi, Mrs. Stephenson. I'm Dr. Charlotte Fairwell. I don't work at this hospital, but I'm a cardiologist in town visiting my grandmother. Is it okay if I check you?" The woman's gaze shifted to her, and she nodded. Lottie placed her finger on the woman's radial pulse and wasn't pleased with the thready, irregular beat beneath the woman's clammy skin. "Do you have a heart condition, Mrs. Stephenson? An arrhythmia or history of angina, maybe?"

Still rubbing her sternum, the woman shook her head. "I don't think so since I don't know what those things are."

Lottie glanced at Linc. "Do you have aspirin or nitroglycerin?"

He shook his head. "Unfortunately, no."

Lottie was afraid of that.

"Mrs. Stephenson, we need to get you to the emergency room," Lottie continued, keeping her voice gentle, but firm.

"I don't want to go." Mrs. Stephenson's voice trembled. "I'll be fine in a minute. This happened earlier and passed. I already feel better just being off the bike. After my knee replacement, I don't need another medical bill."

"I understand that, but you do need an EKG and cardiac enzyme laboratory tests." Lottie leaned forward to place her ear against the woman's chest, listening to the unsteady thumping. "There isn't really a choice." Straightening, she met Linc's gaze. "We need to get her to the emergency room. Do whatever needs to happen to get her there. STAT."

Something Lottie didn't have time to explore shone in his eyes as he nodded. "There's a wheelchair by the reception desk."

"You stay. I'll get the wheelchair," Shannon offered, already back on her feet. "I can take her to the emergency room to have her checked and will give her orthopedic surgeon a call to let him know what's up."

Keeping a finger on Mrs. Stephenson's pulse, Lottie nodded as Shannon left.

"Mrs. Stephenson, at the minimum your heart is out of rhythm." Lottie motioned for Linc to elevate the woman's legs, nodding her approval when he did so. "Linc and I are going to put you into a wheelchair, then we'll get you to the emergency room."

"No." Sweat beaded on Mrs. Stephenson's forehead. "I'm not—okay." She winced, gasping a little. "I'll go. We should probably hurry."

Glad Mrs. Stephenson wasn't going to waste more energy, and perhaps time, protesting, Lottie kept her gaze locked on the woman, who'd closed her eyes. "Mrs. Stephenson?"

"Hmm?" The woman's eyelids fluttered a little but didn't open, not even when Shannon returned with the wheelchair and said her name.

"Are you hurting worse?" Lottie gently shook the woman's shoulder.

Her eyes opened. "I'm dizzy."

"Okay. We're going to help you into the wheelchair." Linc, Lottie and Shannon got the woman into the wheelchair and wrapped a strap around her to secure her in. The last thing they needed was her falling out as they rushed her to the emergency department.

"Let's go," Lottie said the moment they had the strap tightened. She had meant Shannon, but Linc grabbed the wheelchair's handles.

"Finish up another round of sets, Jerry," he called over his shoulder. "You know what to do. I'll be back."

"Will do."

They'd barely made it into the hallway when Mrs. Stephenson said, "I may pass out."

Her head bobbed, pressing her chin into her chest.

Linc stopped pushing the wheelchair. "Mrs. Stephenson?"

Lottie bent, putting her ear to the woman's heart. The beat was there, but weak and irregular. She shook her shoulder, harder than before. "Mrs. Stephenson? Can you hear me, Mrs. Stephenson?"

Nothing. Lottie flattened her palm against the woman's chest, then swore under her breath. The erratic beats had stopped. To Linc, she said, "Help me get her out of the chair and onto the floor. She needs CPR now."

To Shannon, she said, "Call a code and get us help now. We're out of time."

While Shannon made the call, Linc and Lottie lowered Mrs. Stephenson to the floor. Lottie immediately started compressions. Linc got into two-person CPR position and delivered two breaths.

Arms pressing deep into Mrs. Stephenson's chest, Lottie counted out loud, going to thirty, then pausing for Linc to rapidly deliver another two breaths. Lottie started over, delivering the compressions, counting them out loud to help maintain her rhythm and to let Linc know when to give more lifesaving breaths.

"Just tell me if you need me to take over compressions," Linc offered in between breaths.

Lottie nodded. If the code team took much longer, she'd have to take him up on that. Her arms were gelatin from the exhausting movements. Who would have ever guessed that someday she and Linc would be working together to try to save a woman's life? That he'd let her take charge and would do as she asked without question? That he'd look to her with such confidence that she'd know what to do and let her? Brian would have taken over. Not a fair thought. Brian was also a cardiologist. Linc was a physical therapist. Of course he'd let her run the show during a myocardial infarction.

"Oh, God. Please don't let her die," Shannon said from where she fretted near them. Lottie glanced her way long enough to make sure the therapist wasn't going to lose her composure. Linc must have wondered, too, as he motioned for Shannon to sit beside them.

"If anyone can save her, it's Lottie." The pride in his voice was so pure, so strong, that Lottie's gaze shot to his as she continued to compress and count. Pride and something more shone there. Something raw and intense that made her own heart do a funny flip-flop.

It seemed to take forever for help to arrive, but Lottie knew from experience that it really hadn't been more than a few minutes at most.

When the nurse arrived with the crash cart, Lottie continued compressions until the defibrillator was charged and ready to give a two-hundred-joules shock to Mrs. Stephenson's heart.

"All clear," the nurse ordered.

Lottie moved back as the paddles were placed on the woman's chest and delivered the voltage, causing Mrs. Stephenson's body to jerk.

The second the paddles were removed Lottie began compressions again. "One. Two. Three. Four," she said in rapid succession, continuing her count.

"We have a pulse!" the nurse who'd rushed to

them with the crash cart announced. "It's weak, but we have a pulse!"

Lottie kept compressing Mrs. Stephenson's chest, afraid to stop too soon, but relief spread through her when the woman sucked in a breath on her own. *Yes!*

Another hospital employee arrived with a gurney. Lottie stopped compressing, remaining on the floor as Linc and the man lifted Mrs. Stephenson onto the gurney and another of the code team took over rhythmically compressing the woman's chest. Within seconds, she was being rushed down the hallway toward the emergency department.

Lottie's shoulders slumped, and she rubbed her palms over her trembling biceps. She always thought she was in decent physical shape until she had to perform CPR. That never failed to be an eye-opener.

"You okay?" Linc stretched out his hand to help Lottie up.

"Fine, but I'll probably be sore tomorrow." She automatically took his hand so he could assist her back to her feet. The second his hand closed around hers, her insides jerked to life as surely as if he'd hit her with the defibrillator paddles. He must have felt it, too, because as soon as she was standing, he let go and rubbed his palm against his thigh.

"That was unexpected," Shannon said from beside them, no doubt referring to Mrs. Stephenson's heart attack, but as Lottie stared at Linc, she thought he was what was so unexpected. He'd been so wonderful while they'd done CPR, so supportive and perfectly in sync with her compressions.

"Yes, it was." Lottie stuck her hand into her pocket to keep from also rubbing her stinging palm against her thigh. Still staring at him, she swallowed. Why? Why did he have to be in Fripp? She was content with her life in Boston. It was what she'd worked toward, and yet, looking into Linc's blue eyes, everything back home just seemed drab.

"Lottie—" he said, his voice a bit breathy. Was it from what had happened with Mrs. Stephenson or what was sparking between them?

"I've got to go." She couldn't deal with the emotions bubbling inside her, not in front of Linc and his coworker. Maye not ever. "I've got to get to Gram's room." Anywhere to have a few moments to decompress and sort through all the questions that coming face-to-face with Linc again was raising. "She should be there by now. I hope Mrs. Stephenson will be okay." She glanced toward Linc, found him studying her with concerned eyes, and she quickly averted her gaze because her emotions were stretched in a tug-of-war between reason and something akin to hope. But hope for what? She'd reached out to him all those years ago and he'd rejected her. She'd moved on, was in a stale, but safe relationship with a good man. So why did looking at Linc fill her with what-ifs?

"Are you okay?"

Lottie glanced up from where she sat next to her sleeping grandmother's hospital bed. She'd been going through messages, several from Brian wondering when she was coming home, and thinking about the fact that she was responding to other texts but not his.

Linc's dark scrubs intensifying the blue of his eyes, he stood inside the room and watched her in a way that made her wonder how long he'd been standing there.

"Of course. All in a day's work."

"Not in my day's work. It was a stressful situation." One corner of his mouth lifted in a half grin. "I'm glad you were there."

Her heart did a funny pitter-patter thing that she was positive it shouldn't be doing. Funny how a teenage love could still have such an affect. Or maybe it was that Linc was a gorgeous man, and that grin would have had her heart fluttering even if she'd never met him all those years ago. Maybe both was closer to the truth. She clutched her phone tighter.

"You made quite the impression on my patient." Glancing toward where Gram lay in her hospital bed, eyes closed, breathing evenly, Linc came into the room to stand close to where Lottie sat. He kept his voice low. "You're Jerry's hero."

His tone was a mix of admiration and teasing. Lottie's stomach took a cue from her heart and got all jittery. Her phone vibrated in her palm. Although her roommate Camilla's name popped up on the screen, the reminder of the unanswered messages from Brian caused guilt to flicker through her. She should have answered his messages. Why hadn't she?

Brian's the perfect man for you, Charlotte. You're going to have such a great life with him. You make me so proud.

Heart squeezing, Lottie took a deep breath.

Oh, Mama, I miss you so much.

"Mrs. Stephenson was only in the ER a few minutes before they had her in the cath lab. Fortunately, she made it through her stent placement and her doctor thinks she's going to be okay."

That the woman had survived was a true relief.

"I'm glad the nurse arrived with the defibrillator when she did, that Mrs. Stephenson's heart responded and that she was able to get to the emergency room so quickly."

"Thanks to you," Linc said, smiling as he moved closer to where she sat. "I'm with Jerry. You're my hero. I'm proud of you, Lottie, of the woman you've become. I always knew you were destined for great things, but watching you today, well, you hammered home just how amazing that young girl I once knew grew up to be."

Embarrassment replaced her relief. Embarrassment and deep pleasure that Linc was proud of her. Wasn't that what she'd dreamed of for so long? For him to see her and recognize that she'd been worth his giving their long-distance love affair a chance to work? Why had he been so adamant that they cut all ties and then done just that?

"I didn't do anything you wouldn't have done if I hadn't been there." Because despite his having let her do what she needed to do, he'd been calm and she knew he would have gotten Mrs. Stephenson the care she needed. "I was just at the right place at the right time to make me look good."

"Thank God you were." He quietly moved a chair next to hers and sat down. "Emergency medicine isn't my thing."

"Nor mine," she admitted, staring at her sleeping grandmother to keep from looking toward him. He was so close she'd swear she could smell the crisp scent of his soap. Crazy, as it would have been hours ago when he showered. If she looked at him, would he see her inner turmoil? Would he know that seeing him again had everything she'd thought she'd known about her life, her future, up in the air? "My patients are usually fairly stable when I get to them as I do more interventional cardiology than emergent."

He shrugged. "Either way, you impressed me and Jerry. He couldn't stop talking about you."

"Was he offering more dating advice?" Now why had she brought that up? She didn't want to discuss Jerry's misguided thoughts. Or to talk dating with Linc. She didn't have to look his way to know he studied her.

"Just to Shannon." His soft answer had Lottie's gaze cutting toward him. The blue of his eyes burned into her and had her fighting a gulp. "He told her that she'd better up her game since there was competition in town."

Lottie gave in to the gulp.

"That not only were you beautiful, but you're smart and a doctor to boot. I reminded him that although everything he said was true, you were involved with someone so there wasn't competition. He just laughed. Crazy old man." Linc paused. "Like I said, he was quite impressed with how you saved Mrs. Stephenson."

"We saved her," she reminded him, because he'd been right there with her doing the CPR, and to give herself a moment to process that he was involved with the pretty therapist beyond a working relationship. The realization stung. How much she was bothered by the realization stung even more. "Interesting advice. I thought you weren't dating anyone."

His gaze didn't waver from hers. "What you asked me was if there was anyone special in my life."

"To which you said no," she stated, doing her best to keep her gaze locked with his despite struggling with the fact that she had no right to question him, to feel such angst over the idea of him with the woman.

"I told you the truth." Linc's voice was steady, just as his gaze was. His gaze was also curious, no doubt wondering why she pressed him about things that shouldn't matter to her. She agreed. His dating life shouldn't matter. The nausea in her stomach suggested it did.

"You're dating Shannon, but it's not serious?" At least, not on his part. The way the other woman had looked at him suggested she would welcome a serious relationship.

"I'm not dating Shannon. We went to dinner

a few times after I first moved here, but nothing serious and nothing recently."

"Sorry," she said and meant it. "I had no right to pry." Nor should she have felt such a green surge at the thought of him with the woman or the wave of relief that he no longer was. "You'll have to forgive me." She'd obviously lost her mind. "After the excitement in the therapy room, I've sat in silence all afternoon while Gram has slept except for a few waking moments here and there."

His gaze narrowing, he seemed to consider saying something more, but instead glanced toward Gram. "Has Dr. Collins been around? What's he saying about how her surgery went?"

Relieved that he wasn't pressing for why Lottie had pried, an answer she wouldn't have been able to give, she sighed. "That she did great, and he doesn't foresee any complications. If she does well tonight, he's transferring her to a rehabilitation facility tomorrow."

"I'm not going to a nursing home," her grandmother informed them in a firm voice that hinted that she hadn't just awakened.

Lottie's gaze went to the petite woman lying on the hospital bed. Happiness hit at the spunk in Gram's voice. When she'd awakened earlier her voice had been weak, and she'd still been disoriented.

"Ah, so you've been faking it this whole time, leaving me twiddling my thumbs," Lottie accused, wincing a little as she recalled her and Linc's conversation. How much had her grandmother overheard?

"Amazing the things you learn while sleeping." Paler than her bravado would suggest, Gram reached for her bed's controller, pressed the button to raise the bed. "When did you ask Linc if there was someone special in his life?"

Lottie winced. Gram had heard too much.

"Today while I was in the surgery waiting room. He stopped by to check on you." Not answering would just have Gram digging deeper. Better to answer as if the question was no big deal. It wasn't, right? Just as whether or not he was involved in a serous relationship wasn't a big deal? Why couldn't she convince herself of that? Lottie glanced toward Linc. Although unreadable, his features appeared relaxed. "We were catching up while waiting to hear news about your surgery. Asking if there's someone special in one's life is a natural question that friends who haven't seen each other in a long time ask each other."

There. Hopefully that would satisfy her grandmother and, also, let Linc know why she'd asked.

Gram snorted. "Natural if you're still interested in each other."

Lottie shot another apologetic look toward Linc to see how he'd taken Gram's comment. He'd been the one to reject her even after she'd poured out her heart. She hadn't forgotten or forgiven him for that. Not really. Had the way he'd looked at her, teased her, kissed the top of her head, been because he was still interested? And if so, then what? Would she throw away her relationship with Brian, no doubt causing her mother to roll over in her grave, just to risk having her heart shattered again?

"Excuse her." Lottie rolled her finger in a crazy motion. "The anesthesia has affected her. She doesn't know what she's saying."

"I know exactly what I'm saying. Just because I'm trapped in this bed, it does not mean you can get away with saying things such as I'm not in my normal state of mind," Gram overprotested, causing both Lottie and Linc to smile. His smile sent sunshine through Lottie.

"You're right. Sorry, Gram. You're the epitome of brilliance."

"The Einstein of modern days," Linc added, his eyes sparkling.

"Tesla would have been wowed by your supreme intelligence." Lottie loved how Gram's color had brightened from the pasty white of when she'd first awakened.

"I know I'm wowed," Linc continued. "By that and your card playing skills."

Gram harrumphed and Linc chuckled. Lottie had been going to ask how he knew about Gram's card shark ways, but then he winked. Conspiratorially rather than anything overtly romantic, but still, her rib cage contracted around her lungs, taking her breath and momentarily she couldn't do anything other than stare at him in wonder.

Who would have ever thought she'd be in a hospital room teasing her grandmother with Lincoln Thomas? That being near him would put the same excitement in her belly that it had when she'd been eighteen and hadn't had her heart broken by him yet? But she wasn't a teenager anymore and had a life that was so far removed from this room and the girl who had cried herself to sleep for months at his rejection. But with the giddiness filling her at his simplest gestures, maybe she wasn't so far removed from the young girl she'd once been.

"No doubt the Fripp Card Club will be holding new elections while you're incapacitated and will vote you off the island—I mean, club." Linc's lips twitched.

"They wouldn't dare." Stiffening, Gram narrowed her gaze, then, glancing back and forth between them, she relaxed against her pillow. "Look at you two picking on me when I've had a rough couple of days. Not that I'm surprised that y'all fell right into sync just the way you always did."

They had, hadn't they? Not that they'd picked on Gram back in the day. Jackie would have tanned their hides, perhaps rightly so. Still, Gram was right. Even as adults, she and Linc shared a connection that Lottie had never experienced with anyone else.

"That anesthesia really has you not thinking clearly." Maybe there really was some lingering in the air because Lottie didn't feel as if she were thinking clearly, either. If she was, her mother's voice telling her how perfect Brian was for her and to hang on to him no matter what would be playing loudly in her head. Instead, Lottie refused to listen to the voice that she usually welcomed in no matter what words were being said. How could she not when she missed her mother so? But she didn't want to think about Brian or how disappointed her mother would be if she knew what Lottie was feeling while looking at the one and only boyfriend her mother had ever disliked. Had Vivien known Linc had been destined to hurt her?

"My thinking is just fine," Gram countered. "Who's Jerry?"

"The patient I was torturing when Lottie saved a woman's life." Linc tone was full of pride, causing Lottie's gaze to reconnect with his. If she didn't know better, she'd think he felt he had a personal stake in her success. If anything, he'd almost wrecked her to the point she'd wanted nothing more than to curl into a ball and cry her days away.

But she hadn't. She'd done what needed to be done and she'd moved on with her life. Without him. Because that's what he'd chosen. Linc had claimed to love her and yet he'd willingly shattered her.

Gram's brow lifted. "So, you saved a woman, rescued Linc's patient and caught up on his dating life? You've been busy this morning."

"Your granddaughter is a special woman," Linc said to Gram. His eyes remained focused on Lottie, though, almost as if he sensed her inner turmoil. No wonder she liked this adult version of him; he was kind, funny, considerate and physically...well, physically, Linc had always done it for her. Part of her wanted to throw caution to the wind and explore the way being near him made her feel. Yet, another wanted to scream and demand to know why he hadn't loved her as much as he'd claimed.

Not pulling her gaze away, Lottie willed for him to know how much he'd hurt her, that no matter how attracted she was to the man he'd grown into, she was older, wiser and would never again allow anyone the power she'd once given over her heart, Especially not him.

CHAPTER FOUR

"How's our girl today?"

Glancing up from where she had been skimming through a continuing medical education article on her phone while sitting next to her grandmother who was watching an *I Love Lucy* rerun, Lottie's heart rate picked up at the sight of Linc entering her grandmother's hospital room. Had navy scrubs ever looked better? *Wowzers.*

"She's not too good." And neither was Lottie. She didn't want to feel anything when she looked at Linc. Not attraction, not whatever else that was thumping around inside her chest. She wanted it gone as it should have been years ago. Didn't he know this would be easier if he'd just stay away? Why wasn't he?

Gram scowled. "I can answer for myself. It's my foot that's broken, not my vocal cords."

Turning off her phone, Lottie sat up straighter in the semicomfortable chair.

"Aren't you just a ray of sunshine," Linc

teased, coming over to stand by Gram's hospital bed and taking her hand. "What's wrong?"

Gram had a momentary look of repentance. "Rough day."

"Tell me about it."

Gram did just that, explaining how her going home plans had yet again been waylaid by a faulty blood pressure cuff and how Dr. Collins didn't plan to discharge her unless she agreed to go to a rehabilitation facility.

Whether she wanted Linc there or not, Lottie soaked up his gentle tone as he explained how Gram would heal faster with the proper care. The boy she'd loved had grown into a gorgeous, compassionate man.

Almost as if he sensed her thoughts, Linc's gaze met hers. What was he thinking? She wished… No, she didn't wish that. Wishing things where Linc was concerned was off-limits. He was off-limits. Once Gram was out of the hospital, their paths wouldn't even have to cross again.

"Is there something I can do to help you feel better, Jackie?"

"You can convince my granddaughter to stay in South Carolina so Dr. Collins will agree to let me go home, and then you can agree to do my therapy there so they will let me out of this place," she immediately responded, shooting Lottie a pointed look.

No. Tell her no, Lottie mentally demanded.

Linc was saved from answering by a knock at Gram's door. Gram's nurse came in, saw Linc and gave him a big smile prior to addressing her patient. Seriously, was every female employee infatuated with him? Or was it just that Lottie found him so irresistible that she automatically thought every woman must, too? Ugh. Why couldn't he have grown up into some inconsiderate jerk who repulsed her so she'd have tucked memories of their summer together away as a fortunate near miss?

"Oh, hi, Linc. I didn't know you were in here." The pretty brunette's cheeks pinkened, then she smiled at Gram. "Dr. Collins put in orders to get you up in a wheelchair for a while to see how you do with sitting."

Gram's brows vee'd. "Has he forgotten that I've been sitting up in this bed?"

"Not quite the same thing." The nurse turned toward Linc. "Would you mind helping me get her into a chair? You probably already know since you're here, but Dr. Collins also ordered a physical therapy consult for you to do an assessment and start treatment."

"It's never a problem to help with a patient, Amy."

Beaufort hospital wasn't so huge that employees wouldn't know each other, especially those whose paths crossed routinely, yet that Linc and the nurse knew each other's first names triggered another dreaded green surge.

What was wrong with her?

She'd never been the jealous type. Not that summer with Linc and certainly never with Brian.

While Lottie's stomach gnawed at itself, Linc and the nurse got Gram into position sitting on the side of the bed, chatting with Gram and each other as they did so.

"I'm going to let you sit upright for a minute or two, just to acclimate you to being upright. Then, we'll get you into the wheelchair."

Gram huffed out a deep breath, then shook her head. "I don't need a wheelchair."

Lottie disagreed. Even as distracted as she was with watching Linc and Amy, she wasn't so blind to have not noticed how breathy Gram had gotten with the position change.

"Doctor's orders," Amy reminded Gram, doing another quick vital check on her.

Beep. Beep. Beep. Amy's pager sounded. The nurse glanced at it and grimaced.

Lottie stepped closer to her grandmother. "I'll help Linc if you need to take that page."

The nurse looked torn, as if she didn't want

to go, but knew she needed to. After the brief hesitation, she nodded. "Thank you. That would be wonderful as I do need to get this one sooner rather than later." She glanced toward Gram. "How are you feeling? Any light-headedness?"

Too proud to say otherwise, Gram insisted, "I'm fine."

"Great. No worries as you're in good hands with Linc. He's the best therapist in the hospital." She sent Linc a glowing smile to go with her praise. "If you need anything, hit your call button. I'll be back as quickly as I can."

"She's cute, Linc," Gram pointed out after the nurse had left the room. "You should invite her out to the island and cook her one of those yummy shrimp dishes you make."

Lottie fought the urge to place her hand on her forehead. One minute Gram was pushing her and Linc together and the next she was encouraging him to ask a nurse to dinner?

"Is she?" He seemed oblivious as he made sure the locks were on, then positioned the chair to where they could most easily get Gram into it. "I'll keep it in mind, but I doubt she would be nearly as appreciative of my grilled Cajun shrimp as you are."

Lottie blinked. Linc had cooked for her grandmother?

"Then her taste buds are dead. My mouth waters just thinking about them. Sneak me in some. That'll make me feel better."

Moving to the opposite side of where Linc inspected the chair, Lottie filled the spot the nurse had vacated. "I'll let dietary know you'd like shrimp," she offered, "but I bet it's not on their menu due to someone possibly being allergic."

"Poor souls," Gram said, her palms against the bed with her fingers curled around the mattress edge as if she wasn't quite as confident in her strength as she verbalized.

Linc gestured toward the wheelchair. "You ready to transfer?"

Gram nodded and so did Lottie. It had been a while since she'd help transfer a patient, but she'd done so many a time over the years, especially during the early stages of residency.

"I was born ready," Gram assured him, gaining smiles from both Lottie and Linc.

"Great." Linc looked directly into Gram's eyes. "We're going to do this without you putting any weight on your casted foot, okay?"

"Sounds simple."

"It won't be," he stated. "But the main thing is to make sure you don't fall. I want you to put your arm around my neck so I can help support you."

He lowered to where she could more readily reach her arm over his shoulder.

"That's a good line. I bet you say it to all the girls." Gram put her arm around his neck.

"Only the ones I like." He grinned. "How are you feeling? Light-headed?" Linc asked as they helped Gram reposition.

"Like the world is one big merry-go-round."

"I thought that might be the case."

Linc's gentle tone, the way he maneuvered Gram into the chair with ease, and immediately knelt to elevate her casted foot on the footrest had Lottie feeling a little as if she'd joined her grandmother on that merry-go-round. Was his bedside manner this wonderful with all his patients? Having witnessed the teasing rapport with Jerry, she suspected so.

Quit being so wonderful.

"Better?" Linc asked.

Gram nodded, but still looked pale. Linc must have had the same impression, because he stayed in the kneeling position, talking with her for a few minutes prior to straightening.

"I'll log in to see what orders Dr. Collins has written." He glanced at his watch. "I have a therapy session starting in a few minutes, but I'll be back afterward."

When Linc had left, Gram sniffled. "I just want to go home, Lottie. I miss Ole Bessie and Maritime. Please do whatever it takes to get me home."

* * *

"It's true, then? You're staying in South Carolina?"

"Yes." Word had sure traveled fast at Boston Memorial. Gripping her phone tighter, Lottie winced at the unhappiness in Brian's tone.

A nurse aide had come by to change Gram's bedding while she was in her chair, and to give Gram a sponge bath. After the woman had left, Lottie decided to watch a nature program on TV with her grandmother. When her cell phone rang and she'd seen Brian's name, she stepped outside the room to take the call.

"I'm staying until Gram gets steady enough on her feet that I feel comfortable leaving her. Hopefully just a few weeks, but maybe a month or two."

"A month or two?" Brian sounded incredulous. "Can't you hire someone to stay with her? There has to be someone better suited to grandma-sit than someone with your credentials. You have an important job and commitments, Charlotte. You can't just be gone from your life for that long."

"I also have obligations to Gram. I'm all she has." And vice versa. "I want to do this for her. Besides, it was Human Resources that suggested I take a family medical leave." Other than quick trips to see Gram and the occasional vacation,

Lottie never took time off work. She had quite a bit of built-up paid time off she'd thought to put to good use staying with Gram, but the HR manager had advised her to pursue short-term leave for a couple of months, stating Lottie could return sooner but that would cover her just in case. "Greg Abbott even called not long afterward. He understands that I need to be here right now."

Which was saying more than Brian. Seriously? Could she hire someone to sit with Gram? This wasn't about money. It was about family and taking care of one's family.

"It would seem I'm the last to know."

"That wasn't my intention, Brian. You were with patients this morning, so I texted and asked you to give me a call when you had a free moment. I didn't want to interrupt something important," she replied, frustrated that she was having to defend the desire to take care of Gram. No, he and Gram didn't jibe, but Gram was her only living relative. He knew that. Shouldn't he be showing some concern? Some empathy and understanding of why she'd want to be there?

"You could have texted more details."

"I thought it was something I should tell you in person."

There was a pause, and then he sighed. "Do you know how embarrassing it is that the receptionist whom I corrected when she said how sorry she was that you were having to take an extended leave to take care of your ill grandmother was actually correct and knew more than I did?"

Was that the real problem? Not that Lottie hadn't told him, nor that she wasn't coming home, but that he'd been embarrassed?

"I knew my patients would need to be rescheduled and wanted to give HR as much of a heads-up as possible."

She and Brian had been together for over five years. She understood his point. She should have given him more details in her text, possibly, but she hadn't counted on the grapevine getting to him first. He was frustrated, and wouldn't she have been if the situation had been reversed?

No, because you'd have been with him. You'd have set everything aside and gone to South Carolina to help in any way you could, even if it was just emotional support.

Which wasn't a fair thought since he was helping by taking the overflow of her patient load.

"I'm sorry that you're upset, Brian, but I promised Gram I'd stay as long as she needed me and that's what I intend to do." Seeing her grandmother so broken earlier had done Lottie in. She'd have promised her the moon if it had meant drying the unshed tears in Gram's eyes.

"And it doesn't matter if I need you here?"

His question surprised Lottie. These days they rarely interacted during work hours, not even making time to grab lunch together. When had they stopped doing that? Why hadn't she noticed? She enjoyed when they were together, but was that because they were mostly with their friends or with Lottie's roommate, Camilla? How long had it even been since they'd done more than a quick peck to the lips? Not that she'd ever felt great passion at his touch, but shouldn't her feelings be something more than lukewarm?

"Do you need me there, Brian?"

Was his long hesitation due to his frustration at having heard that she was taking family medical leave from someone else or that he really had to think that hard to know the answer?

Why did knowing his answer seem so imperative? Did Brian need her there? Did he need her at all? Did she need him? Or were they just together out of habit and an affection for one another than kept them from not wanting to cause the other pain? Why did her stomach squeeze so tightly as she contemplated questions that she suspected had been there a long time, but that she hadn't wanted to deal with the ramifications of asking? Brian was who her mother thought was the perfect husband for her. Her father had liked him. Why was Lottie even questioning his role in her life?

"We'll talk later. I've got patients waiting," he finally said, which really didn't give Lottie resolution to the questions swirling through her mind.

"I—okay." Maybe he'd had a rough morning. Maybe she'd had a rough morning, because her own annoyance and discontent with their current status quo wasn't abating.

Likely, it was being here, in South Carolina, having seen Linc again that made everything back in Boston seem less sparkly. She liked her job, the apartment she shared with Camilla, her usually undemanding relationship with a man she respected and admired—usually.

"He never asked how Gram was." Mumbling, she turned to go back into the hospital room. As she did so, her gaze lit on the man standing a few feet away. "Linc!"

"Sorry, I didn't mean to eavesdrop, but you were deep in conversation and looked upset, so I didn't want to interrupt." His gaze searched hers, for what she wasn't sure, nor was she sure she wanted him to find it. "Dr. Collins did get Jackie's PT ordered so I'm back to do her assessment and get started."

Realizing she had been leaning against the

closed door of her grandmother's room, she grimaced. "Sorry I had the door barricaded."

"Making sure Jackie doesn't escape?"

Appreciative that he hadn't questioned her about her phone conversation, she half smiled. "I'm not sure both of us blocking her door could do that at whatever point she decides she's had enough. I should probably get in there before she climbs out the window."

Although lingering concern swirled in his eyes, he chuckled. "You're right, but short of Jackie busting it, you're safe on a window escape since they don't open. How did she do with sitting in the wheelchair after I left? Any lightheadedness?"

Was he intentionally repeating his question to ask how Gram was? Had he heard Lottie's grumbled complaint that Brian hadn't asked? Or was that her mind connecting dots where dots didn't exist? And why would she connect dots where Linc was concerned? She didn't want to like him. Lord, her insides were a jumbled mess.

"She seems tired. The nurse aide came by to change her bedding and bathe her. I imagine that's worn Gram out even more. But other than in protest of being kept here, she's determined to not utter a word of complaint about actual symptoms for fear that Dr. Collins will decide that she can't leave tomorrow."

"You think he's going to discharge her with her wanting to go home instead of to a rehab facility? That's why you've decided to stay longer?"

So, he had heard at least that much.

"I hope not since I'll be the one having to handle her at home. I don't want Gram miserable, but I also want her taken care of to where she can heal properly without falling or reinjuring herself because I didn't do something right."

"You being here is right enough, Lottie." Oh, how his words spread balm over her raw nerves. "If she hasn't told you, then I'll say it for her. She's ecstatic you're here." He gave her an empathetic look. "As far as once you do get her home, I'm just down the street if you need help."

Knowing his offer was genuinely given, Lottie wondered just how long she was going to be able to hold on to her inner anger. Seriously, why did this adult Linc have to be so great? "Thank you."

"No problem. I'm at your service, have duct tape and make a credible alibi." He waggled his brows. "What more could you need?"

The tension in her shoulders eased. "I'll keep that in mind if she gets too out of line."

Memories of his helping Gram with dozens of things around her home that long ago summer popped into Lottie's head. Based on what she could tell, they'd picked back up on that with his moving to Fripp. He and Gram had always gotten along. Too bad her parents hadn't thought much of her summer infatuation with a construction worker. They'd loved Brian, though. Her mother had often commented on what beautiful grandbabies she and Brian's upper-middle-class parents would someday have. Lottie had always smiled, nodded, assumed that someday she and Brian would marry and have those grandchildren her mother mentioned. But for the life of her she couldn't picture those brown-eyed children her mother had described. Closing her eyes, she tried, but instead saw blue-eyed, sunkissed imps with dimpled grins smiling up at her and wrapping her around their adorable fingers.

Startled at the vision, Lottie forced the image from her head, sucked in a deep breath and met the bluest eyes she'd ever looked in to. Heart pounding, she glanced away, scared he'd see what had been in her mind. It didn't take a genius to know who those imaginary kids had looked like. What was wrong with her? Obviously, she was having a stress reaction to having her life upheaved by Gram's fall and coming face-to-face with Linc after all this time.

"I'm serious, Lottie. If you need something, I'll be there."

She'd once needed him, and he hadn't been

there. But he'd meant for Gram. Despite his kindness and the way his gaze lingered at times, Linc didn't have feelings for her anymore. Nor did she want him to. Not in any way more than the way that was normal for you to want your exes to see you and wonder why they ever let you go.

"When Dr. Collins lets her go home, I would appreciate help in getting her into the house." And so many other things if her grandmother wasn't able to hobble around on crutches. Avoiding Linc would make Lottie's life easier, but Gram came first. "Can you imagine me trying to get her up those steps and into the house?"

He grimaced. "Don't attempt it, Lottie. It's not worth the risk of her falling and injuring herself further. I'll get her inside."

He was right. It wasn't worth the risk of attempting to do things without his help. At whatever point Dr. Collins discharged Gram, she'd enlist him to get Gram into the house. Once there, hopefully, Lottie could manage the rest.

Leaning back against the wall, Lottie sighed. "Stubborn woman. Things would be so much simpler if she'd go to rehabilitation. But other than the circumstances, spending a few weeks with her on the island isn't such a tough pill to swallow."

His eyes softened, then averting his gaze, he glanced at his watch. "I better get started."

Lottie stepped aside, meaning to go into Gram's room with him, but her phone buzzed. Thinking it was likely Brian to say he was sorry for his earlier attitude, she glanced at the screen. Camilla. Good. She hadn't wanted to talk to Brian again anyway. Not unless he really had been calling to apologize.

Men. Maybe she was finished with the whole lot of them.

Lottie had sat with her grandmother until Jackie dozed off. After getting back to "Ole Bessie," she'd thought she'd sleep herself as she was at a deficit for the past few nights. That was saying something because she never got much rest. Yet now that she'd picked up Maritime from Mrs. Baker's house and could sleep until the next morning, restless energy stole her slumber. Rather than uselessly lying in her bed, she sat in the covered porch's swing and stared toward the canal. Reflections from the homes on the other side of the water twinkled, and an occasional shadow passed by a lit window.

It wasn't that late, barely nine, but still, she should be exhausted. She was exhausted. And yet her mind raced. She knew why, so didn't bother trying to delve into the reasons she couldn't sleep. Her mother had thought Brian the perfect man for her, but Lottie wasn't so sure. Maybe she never had been. He had called and apologized, but Lottie had cut the conversation short rather than say the things wanting to burst free from her. Things like, *Let's just be friends*.

No, you can't do that.

Sighing at her mother's voice, wishing she could hear it for real, rather than just echoes from the past, Lottie grabbed her shoes. Maybe a walk to the beach and back would help.

"Woof!"

Lottie winced. Taking the dog with her would significantly decrease odds of having a peaceful walk, and yet with the dog's expectant look and knowing she'd likely been cooped up inside Mrs. Baker's for most of the day, Lottie couldn't bring herself to not take her.

"Fine. I'll bring you." She hooked Maritime's leash to her collar, and for once the dog cooperated. "Good job."

The moment they stepped outside, the dog bounded down the stairs and waited impatiently while Lottie undid the gate's lock. As she lifted the latch, she gave Maritime a stern look. "We'll walk to the beach and back, but you have to be quiet. No barking."

The dog let loose a few loud barks in response. Lottie rolled her eyes and gave the leash a firm tug. "Shush. It's not too late for me to change my mind, you know? I don't know what Gram sees in you."

The dog gave another loud bark. Lottie suspected if she could interpret the sound it would translate to something along the lines of Maritime didn't know what Gram saw in Lottie, either, other than that they were blood related and Gram couldn't really help that. But rather than more barked protests, Maritime fell into step beside Lottie as they took off down the paved road that ran in front of Gram's and led to the beach.

The ocean cut through the silence of the night.

When she walked past the McMahon place, Maritime tugged on her leash.

"Stop that," Lottie ordered, but the dog continued to pull, hard, and began to bark. Scanning the dimly lit house's yard, Lottie didn't see anything warranting Maritime's ruckus. "It's probably just a deer, you silly girl. Stop barking."

She tugged on the leash, trying to prompt the dog to continue their walk, but Maritime wasn't giving in.

Lottie stepped a few feet into the driveway, loosened the length of the leash to give the dog more room to wander and hoped that would satisfy Maritime's curiosity. At least, she'd stopped barking. While the dog sniffed the ground beneath a palmetto tree, Lottie glanced toward the house again. What was Linc up to?

None of your business, she told herself. *Go, walk to the beach, sit in the sand and watch the moonlight shimmer on the water.*

She'd had no idea what Linc had been up to for twelve years. She didn't need to know now, either.

"Hurry up," she told the dog, but Maritime didn't even turn her way, just took off toward the freshly painted gate that led to the stairway and on to the elevated porch entrance to Linc's house. As the leash length ended, the dog came to a halt, then began his barking again.

"Shush, Maritime," Lottie ordered, pulling on the leash. She didn't want the noise alerting Linc that she was there.

Still barking, Maritime gave another tug on the leash and managed to pull free from Lottie's hold.

"Get back here," she called as Maritime eluded her attempts to recapture the leash. Instead, the dog jumped up, used her nose to undo the gate's latch and bounded up the steps. "No!"

Lottie took off after the dog. "Get back here now. See if I ever take you on another walk."

Pawing at the front door, Maritime took to barking, again.

"Got you!" Lottie announced, grabbing hold

of the leash. "Don't expect to sleep in my room tonight. If not for Gram, you'd be toast." Not looking as if she believed Lottie, Maritime gave a yelp of protest as Lottie practically dragged all sixty uncooperative pounds of her back down the porch steps. "Stop. We're going home. And you have no one but yourself to blame when I go on future walks without you."

She'd just reached the gate, when the front door opened and Maritime launched a renewed and noisy effort to make her way back up the steps.

"Lottie?"

Bark. Bark. Bark.

"Maritime, please be quiet." Amazingly, the dog listened. She not only stopped barking but plopped down on her behind as she stared up toward the porch. Giving the dog a look that she hoped conveyed that she was on to her, Lottie then glanced up. Linc had come out onto the porch and stood at the railing. Wearing only shorts, he stood there silhouetted by the house's lights. Broad shoulders and chiseled pecs narrowed down to his slim waist and hips. Good grief, he was beautiful. Lottie swallowed. Would Maritime rein her in if she took off up the stairs in a heated pant?

Having spent his days doing hard, manual labor on a construction site day after day, Linc had had a fit body at nineteen. But nothing that compared to how he'd filled out; he was simply perfect now. Lottie's hand gripping the leash grew clammy. Ha! Despite the ocean breeze whipping around her, her whole body had grown clammy.

"Is everything okay?"

No. Everything was not okay. Far, far from it. The past few days had completely unraveled the anger that had gotten her through the past twelve years, and all that was left was confusion. How could she look at him and want him so badly when she knew he'd never loved her the way she'd once loved him?

"What are you doing here, Lottie?"

Great question. Knowing she was fighting a losing battle, she shrugged. "Would you believe the dog dragged me?"

"I might." Amusement laced his words. "Do you want to see the house?"

Maritime answered for her, jerking the leash free of Lottie's sweaty hand and taking off up the stairs.

As her inner jitteriness grew with each step, she prayed, *Lord, please don't let this be a mistake.*

CHAPTER FIVE

WAS HE COMPLETELY CRAZY? Linc wondered as he knelt to scratch Maritime behind the ears. Inviting Lottie inside his house was nothing short of certifiable.

He'd never had a heartbreak like the one he'd had at her hands. Not that she'd intentionally hurt him. She hadn't. All she'd done was change the course of his destiny one summer long ago. She'd changed him that summer.

For the better. Not that he'd known it at the time. He'd just known that he'd let someone special slip through his fingers because deep down he'd known her mother was right. He hadn't been good enough for Lottie, not then. As the years past, he'd convinced himself that he'd built up Lottie in his mind to pure goddess status and that was why she still haunted his dreams, why he'd catch himself comparing women to her memory.

Maybe that's what had driven him to want

to settle on Fripp, to buy the house she'd once loved. Whatever, inside this house had been the first time he'd had a sense of peace, a sense of belonging somewhere, a sense of finally being good enough. For what, he hadn't been sure since he hadn't seen Lottie in years, but he had felt better than he had since…since Lottie had left Fripp to achieve her lofty life goals. And she had. He'd achieved some lofty life goals, too.

What would her mother say if she were meeting him now for the first time? He'd made a small fortune flipping properties and getting lucky on a few property investments. He no longer had to work, but loved helping others. Would Vivien look at him and still see someone unworthy of her daughter? Or would she embrace him the way she had the cardiologist?

"Hi." Lottie sounded a little breathy, or maybe it had just been the way the wind caught her words making them seem so. Just as the wind, making its way onto the porch, was toying with her hair, making it dance about her head.

"Hi yourself," he said back, moving aside to let her into his house and suddenly feeling self-conscious of his home. "Just remember it's still a work in process. For the most part, I've focused on a few rooms, finishing them, but feel as if I've barely begun with the changes I plan to make to others."

"Oh, I love the kitchen." She moved past him and headed straight to the granite countertop, running her palm across it. "This is gorgeous."

Pride filled him. He'd picked the granite slab himself and had it cut and transported to the island. "Thanks."

She turned. "I take it you started with the kitchen?"

He shrugged. "A man has to eat."

At his comment, her gaze lowered, running over his bare upper body. A blush rose in her cheeks and she hurriedly glanced away, commenting something else about the countertop, he thought, but wasn't sure as his brain had lagged on how Lottie had looked at him.

With interest. Female interest. Which was highly interesting since she was the one in a serious relationship. That phone call hadn't sounded as if it were going well, though. Maybe Lottie wasn't as happy as she'd wanted him to think.

She doesn't have a ring on her finger. The guy was an idiot not to have scooped Lottie up years ago.

Which meant what? That Linc thought he was also an idiot? That maybe they'd been given this second chance for a reason? To see where their relationship would have taken them had they been older and at a different phase of life? He struggled with that. To his knowledge, he'd never intentionally made a move on another man's woman even if that woman felt as if she belonged with him instead.

Aside from the guy in Boston, she had a job, an important job that she loved, in the city. She'd be leaving in a few weeks, and they'd be back to where they'd been all those years ago.

Not quite. Vivien was no longer there reminding him that he had to do the right thing.

The thought made his head spin, just as the fact that Lottie was here, inside his house, had his knees weak.

Needing a moment, he knelt to show Maritime more love. "Hey, girl." He scratched her favorite spot behind her ears. "Who's a good girl?"

"Not her," Lottie said, shaking her head. "We were supposed to be walking to the beach, not making a detour. She wasn't having it and refused to move past your place."

Hands still rubbing Maritime, he glanced up, met Lottie's green gaze and revealed way more than he should. "Like I said, good girl."

Eyes widening she studied him a moment, not with disgust or disapproval, but more with the same confusion he felt. When she finally did speak, she'd steered the conversation away from anything personal, which was perhaps for the best. "So, you started the remodel in the kitchen. What was next?"

"My bedroom." And there he went taking it right back to personal. And that particular personal was too much for him to deal with. He wasn't taking Lottie into his bedroom. Doing so would have him forgetting everything except begging to discover the lovely woman before him, letting her replace old memories. Yeah, they needed to stay out of the bedroom. "I was working in the main bathroom when I heard Maritime at the door. Some buddies and I hung drywall in a few rooms a few days ago, and I've been taking it room by room to putty, sand and paint. I'd planned to get at least the first coat on that bathroom tonight."

"You're working tonight after working twelve hours today?"

He shrugged. "It's a labor of love. Besides, who are you to talk, little Miss Take-a-Walk-at-Night?" Which he really didn't like. The island entrance had a guard shack, but there were a lot of people coming and going with short-term rentals. "Next time you feel the need to go for a walk after dark, call and I'll go with you."

"I was fine," she assured him. "With Maritime to protect me, what could go wrong?"

The dog glanced toward her, then nuzzled her head against Linc's hand. "I'd still feel better if you weren't out walking by yourself after dark."

An amused light shone in her eyes as she

arched a brow. "You didn't mind when I used to sneak out after dark to meet you."

Linc swallowed the lump that formed in his throat at just why Lottie snuck out, where they'd go, what they'd do, and yet as powerful as those memories were, it was the woman before him that he saw, that had his breath catching. "I was a kid who didn't know any better and had ulterior motives to wanting you to sneak out back then." He wanted the brilliant woman she'd become just as much, more even, but never at risk of her safety. "Come on. Let me show you the rest of the house."

Perhaps not sure how to take his comment, probably because his frustration with himself was coming out, she said, "I, uh, okay. Thank you, then I'll let you get back to work."

"And finish your walk?"

"I guess that depends on Maritime. She seems to think she's in charge, so getting her to go down to the beach area might be difficult if that's not where she wants to go."

"She's looking pretty content right here."

"That's because you've been loving all over her since we got here. Who can blame her for not wanting to leave?"

Lottie's lower lip stuck out in a pout, drawing Linc's gaze to her mouth. He wanted to kiss her, to suck that lip into his mouth and gently nip it between his teeth, to taste her sweetness.

Trying to clear the images from his mind, he asked, "Jealous?"

Yes, but Lottie wasn't telling Linc that. Especially not after his comment about being a kid and not knowing any better. Had he meant that as his not knowing better than to mess around with her or that he hadn't known any better on the safety of her sneaking out? She'd never felt unsafe on Fripp. Not then and she hadn't tonight.

At least, not due to anything except how her own body betrayed her.

How else could she describe how being inside the McMahon place—Linc's home—messed with her senses? Ha. It wasn't the house messing with her senses.

Maybe she should tell Linc to put on a shirt. Or two or three. A parka, even.

He should cover up those feet, too. Not that she usually found feet sexy, but there was something about his bare toes that got to her. Maybe memories of playing in the sand and surf with him.

Or memories of rubbing against those feet with her own when—

"I'd love to see the rest of the house," she said in a rush, not letting her thoughts play out. With her comment she took off, startling Maritime who gave a loud, annoyed bark.

"Sure thing." Straightening, Linc followed her. "Had you been in the house before? Back when the McMahons lived here?"

"I peeped in the windows once, but had never been inside," she admitted. "I just wanted to know what the inside of the house looked like but couldn't really tell much beyond the living area on the bottom level. I remember they had it decorated with old movie posters."

"The family moved all those things out. I have workout equipment down there now."

That explained a lot. Those arms. The shoulders. She swallowed. Those abs. Maybe even the calloused hands.

"You're welcome to use it while on the island."

His body?

Hoping he couldn't read her thoughts, she took a deep breath. "Gram will be workout enough once she's home. She ran me crazy the last time I visited. I can only imagine how it's going to be during her recovery."

"When was that?"

"I flew out for a long weekend at Christmas. I tried to convince her to come to Boston so we'd have more time together, but she refused."

"Leave a sunny South Carolina island to go

to blustery cold Boston?" He clicked his tongue. "How did she ever manage to say no?"

Lottie's lips twitched. "You have a point, but at least she'd have had a white Christmas."

He didn't look impressed. "Sand's white."

She laughed. "You don't see many holiday ads promoting that as what is meant as a 'white Christmas.' At least, not outside the travel industry. But I admit that coming here for a few days during the cold was a nice break." She smiled wryly. "I hate the circumstances but being here is nice. I miss her."

"She misses you, too." His empathetic look dug deep within her. "She talks about you."

Lottie's brow rose. "To you? What does she say?"

His face color heightened, as if he realized what he'd said and wished he could take the admission back. "Mainly, she mentions how busy you are and that she worries that you work too much. I think it's after you've talked."

"We text some during the week, but I always call her on Sunday mornings. It's our time. Sometimes things come up at the hospital that delay what time we talk, but we always talk."

Those brief Sunday morning calls with her grandmother were each week's highlight.

"Jackie stops by here a few minutes every

Sunday to check on the house's progress and for a cup of coffee when she walks Maritime."

Hearing her name, the dog cocked her head toward him, wagged her tail, then moved closer for another round of attention. Linc didn't hold back but lavished the dog with a good rub.

No wonder the dog knew to go to his place and was so familiar with him. Not once had her grandmother mentioned Linc in the months since he had moved to the island, but she was obviously repeatedly mentioning Lottie to him. Why hadn't Gram told her he was back? Had Gram purposely been holding back that knowledge? Of course, she had. Question was, why? Had Gram worried Lottie would find excuses not to return to Fripp if she knew Linc was there?

Realizing he was eyeing her oddly, probably because she'd yet to respond to his comment, Lottie smiled. "I'm glad there's so many people on the island who she knows. She has so many friends here who are practically family. Most of my life, I thought Mrs. Baker was blood related, as she had me call her Aunt Mary from the moment I first met her."

"The all-the-timers are definitely a family."

"You're one of them now," she mused. Who would have thought the young teen boy who'd come to Fripp to work would someday live there?

"Yep. I've no plans to go anywhere. Fripp is home and its residents are family. I see myself staying here for the rest of my days. Come on. Let me show you the rest of my house."

Although much of it was in a state of remodel disarray, Lottie loved the insides of the McMahon place. Entering each room, she'd envisioned how it must look with the sunlight coming through the windows, with the view of the ocean waves, and how gorgeous it would be when Linc finished.

When they came to the bathroom he'd been working in, she eyed the painter's tape. "So, this is what I have been keeping you from?"

"It is." Leaning against the doorjamb, he nodded. "Pretty sure you should stay and help make up for it."

His tone was teasing, but Lottie nodded. "I can do that."

"I was joking, Lottie."

"I know, but I'm serious. I've never painted but I'm willing to learn if you're willing to teach." Why was she trying to convince him to say yes? It was better for them both if she just left. "I usually catch on to new things quickly."

"I remember that about you."

Her breath catching, Lottie's gaze locked

with his. "What else do you remember about me, Linc?"

"That you get cranky when you're hungry."

Lottie couldn't argue with that.

"That you love to run to where the waves lap at your feet, turn your face up to the sun and hold your arms out as if you're offering yourself to Poseidon." He painted a memory so vivid that Lottie could almost feel the warmth upon her face and the cold sea at her feet.

"I haven't done that in years," she admitted, wondering at the urge to run out to the water's edge and do so that very moment, embracing the moonlight rather than the sunshine.

"Part of me longs for the girl I was that summer." That was normal, wasn't it? To wish for days that had been stress free? For when she and Linc had been so enthralled with each other that little else had mattered? She shrugged. "Life seemed so perfect back then."

"Maybe it was." His tone was low, but she heard him, heard that bit of yearning for days gone past that she also felt. She also heard the acceptance that that time had long ago passed.

"Look at me now, spending my beach nights offering to help a friend paint." Knowing she needed to get her brain back on track, she picked up a brush and waggled her brows. "Show me what to do."

Thirty minutes later and wearing one of Linc's old T-shirts and drawstring shorts pulled tight so she wouldn't get paint on her clothes, Lottie stroked the brush back and forth, taking pleasure in seeing the dull primer brighten with the paint.

Glancing over at where Linc cut the section around the ceiling, she bit into her lower lip. He'd put on a shirt when he'd given her the clothes to change into, but with his arms stretched above his head, the hem rode up, revealing slivers of toned flesh that somehow had her mouth going bone-dry and watering at the same time.

"Hey, Lottie?"

She dragged her gaze away from that tempting bit of abs. "Um?"

"Painting works better when your brush actually touches the wall."

"What? Oh." She glanced at the brush she held. He was right. She'd been wagging it back and forth in air strokes. How embarrassing. She shook her head.

Looking amused, he knelt next to her. "Here. Let me show you again." He took her hand into his and guided the brush back and forth along the wall, white covering gray.

Skin tingling at where he held her hand, Lottie made light of her own faux pas. "Oh, so that's how this works. Brush against the wall. Got it."

Still gripping her hand, his thumb stroked

across her skin. Breath catching, Lottie watched the gentle movement that was awakening a hurricane of emotion. Slowly, surely, the caress continued until she couldn't resist looking at him.

As she turned his way, he was close. So very close. She could feel his breath against her lips, could see the storm clouds brewing in his eyes as their gazes met. His thumb stilled and his hand trembled. Or maybe it was her hand that trembled. Her gaze dropped to his lips.

She wanted him. This wonderful, thoughtful man, but even as she felt herself lean into him, a voice reminded her that she shouldn't, couldn't kiss him.

Perhaps he thought the same thing because in that same moment his grip on her hand tightened, bringing the brush up and across the tip of her nose.

"Linc!" she sputtered, automatically reaching up to touch the wet paint.

"What?" he asked, grinning.

"Don't you know that painting works best when the brush actually touches the wall?"

"You don't say? Guess we better get back to it, then."

Nodding, Lottie focused on the wall where she'd been working, but the moment he was back in position, stretched to finish up the far corner of where the wall met the ceiling, that sliver of flesh caught her eye. Without letting herself overthink her actions, she pretended to be turning to get more paint, but instead wielded the brush as a weapon and swiped it across the exposed flesh.

Surprise lighting his eyes, he glanced at his stained flesh and T-shirt, then at her. "Forget where the wall was again?"

"Maybe."

He moved closer. "Perhaps you need me to show you again?"

"Perhaps." Lottie's heart beat faster. "Are you going to? Show me, that is?"

"More like I'm going to give you a lesson on what not to do." With that he dabbed his brush at her.

"No," she squealed, scooting away from him. "Uncle. Uncle. I'll behave."

"Sure, you will." He dabbed the paint again, but Lottie was ready and dabbed back, leaving a wide white streak across his face. "That's it. This means war."

A dabbing paint scuffle ensued that had Lottie laughing so hard her sides hurt as she twisted and turned to protect her face and make a play for his at the same time.

Maritime barked excitedly outside the bathroom door, pawing to get in.

"We should stop. She's going to scratch your

door," Lottie warned when Linc had captured both her wrists and held them above her head, having her at his mercy.

Eyes twinkling, he stared at her a moment, seeming torn on whether he wanted to cover her in paint, kiss her, or save his door from Maritime.

"Linc?" she prompted in a voice that was breathy, whether from their scuffle or from how he was looking at her she wasn't sure.

First taking her brush, he lowered her wrists. "You're right. We should stop. Maritime, calm down. I'll be out in a minute to take you outside."

Taking off his T-shirt, he used it to wipe off the bigger paint globs from her face, then his own. "I'll get you a towel."

"Be careful not to track paint through your house," she warned as he went to open the bathroom door.

He paused, grinned. "Now, you're worried about getting paint everywhere?"

Feeling lighter than she had in longer than she could remember, she shrugged. "Better late than never."

Which had her stopping to wonder to just what she was referring to.

"Do we pull off the tape now?"

"Not yet." Glancing at where, paintbrush in

hand, Lottie sat on the floor, Linc tapped the lid back onto a paint can.

Linc would have knocked out painting the bathroom much quicker had he not had his helper, but laughing and playing with Lottie had felt right. After putting on a clean T-shirt and taking Maritime outdoors for a bathroom break, he'd turned on the music that he'd silenced when he'd heard the doorbell, fiddling with his phone until a station with songs from the previous decade played over the house's Bluetooth connected speaker system. They'd sang along with the tunes, laughing at each other repeatedly going off-key while they'd finished coating the walls.

"We'll let the paint dry, then we'll run a putty knife along the edges before pulling up the tape."

Disappointment showed on Lottie's paint-splattered face. "We have to wait for the paint to dry? I'd hoped to see the finished product."

"You can swing by the next time you're out walking Maritime."

"Speaking of Maritime, she and I should head back to Gram's."

What she said was true, but he didn't want her to go. Spending time with her tonight had been…nice. "Want me to give you a ride back?"

She shook her head. "It's not that far. I'll walk."

When Lottie got up from where she'd been working, she stretched, the motion revealing a slim line of pale skin as the hem of his tied T-shirt rose. Desire to place his lips there punched Linc so hard that he had to force himself to look away. What was it about Lottie that kept him on sexual edge anytime she was near?

He took her brush, dropping it, along with the brush he'd used prior to rolling the walls, into a plastic bag, then sealed it. He'd clean them later.

"Come on, girl," he told the dog, going into the kitchen and, with unsteady hands, grabbed her leash off the island. Time had gotten away from them. It was late. He was tired. Lottie was a beautiful woman. He needed to keep his brain on track rather than where it had gone because thoughts of kissing Lottie all over needed to be tamped down. "Ready to go outside, Mari?"

When he straightened from attaching the snap hook to Maritime's collar, Lottie joined him in the kitchen, her face freshly scrubbed. He didn't look her way, couldn't look her way. Letting himself would be inviting trouble. She must have felt the same because he could feel her hesitancy.

"I shouldn't have stayed so late on a weeknight. Sorry." A mixture of apology and uncertainty laced her words. "Thank you for showing me your home and being kind when I offered to stay when you knew I would be more hindrance than help. I'll head home."

He followed her to the door. "You know I'm not letting you walk home alone at this hour, right?"

"Which means that you'd be the one walking home alone." She arched a brow and mimicked, "You think I'd let you walk home alone at this hour?"

Despite his inner turmoil, Linc's lips twitched. "There is that. Let me grab my shoes."

When he returned to the living room, she stood on the front porch, Maritime's leash in hand, staring up at the sky as if it were the most fascinating thing she'd ever seen.

"Thanks for waiting."

She didn't avert her gaze from up above. "You thought I wouldn't?"

"I wondered," he admitted. "You've never been afraid to take off on your own."

He hadn't meant his comment as a reference to when she'd left for Boston, or even when she'd first come to Fripp against her parents' wishes, but as soon as the words left his mouth and her eyes cut to him, he realized that's how she'd taken them.

"It would seem that way." Sighing, she gave in to Maritime's tugging against the leash to hurry down the stairway. When they reached the bottom, she stopped just inside the gate, then turned to where he'd followed. "You really don't have to walk me home, Linc."

They'd had a good time. Obviously, his comment had triggered walls to slide into place. Reaching past her, he lifted the gate latch and pushed the gate open. "I don't have to, but it's the right thing to do."

But rather than take off out the gate, she stood there, eyeing him. "Do you always do the right thing, Linc?"

"Not always and never easily." Take when they'd almost kissed. Only at the last moment had he dabbed her with the paintbrush instead of kissing her until they'd both been breathless. Lottie wasn't free, but it was more than just making moves on another man's woman. It was Lottie giving him the right to be interested in her, in her admitting that she wanted his interest, that she wanted a second chance with him.

"You know…" She looked his way and smiled. "We could just keep walking each other back and forth so the other doesn't have to walk alone."

"We could, but something else I recall about you is that you get pretty grumpy if you don't get your sleep. Since you're picking up Jackie in the morning, I think we'd better get you home and then I'll see myself back to my place and be done with it."

"Ha, that's something else that's changed. Medical school, especially residency, got me over my lack of sleep grumpiness. These days it's a great night if I get six hours."

Linc inhaled a deep breath. The night air carried the salty tang of ocean. "You give the impression that Jackie is right in thinking you work too much, Lottie."

They covered several yards prior to her answering.

"I do work a lot," she admitted. "There's so much to be done and never enough time. We're talking people's lives, so it's not easy to just walk away at the end of the day."

Sensing that she was lost in her thoughts, Linc walked silently beside her, not surprised when after a few moments she continued.

"Plus it only makes sense that I would choose to work a lot. I went to school a long time. It would be a shame not to make the most of all those years of studying and that lack of sleep we were just discussing. Giving up all that snooze time has to be justified, right?"

Her tone was light, but her words held depth, as if she were trying to convince herself of their validity.

"Makes sense, but also makes for an off-balance life."

"I have a great life in Boston," she assured him, her expression, barely visible in the moonlight, challenging him to say otherwise.

Her claim was still playing through Linc's head as they headed up Jackie's driveway. She liked her life. So, what if she and Boston Brian weren't as cozy as he'd initially thought. That didn't change the fact that she'd only be in South Carolina for a short time.

"I feel as if I should ask you up, offer you a drink. Something to be hospitable after you took the time to walk me home." She lingered at Ole Bessie's gate. "Thank you, Linc. I've never been skittish on Fripp. But it was nice not being alone."

"It was the least I could do after you helped me paint."

Her laughter was genuine. "Ha! We both know I got more paint on you than on the wall. Fortunately, white looks good on you."

"On me, you, the floor, a little on the walls," he teased, wondering if the moonlight had ever sparkled so brightly in a woman's eyes.

"Hey, I thought it looked great when we finished."

"We'll know once I pull the tape." He'd never

thought a bathroom would be his favorite room in the house, but after tonight, it might.

"Thanks for teaching me the basics. I doubt I'll ever personally tackle painting a room at my apartment, but if I do, now I know how. My roommate, Camilla, would be so impressed."

Which was a harsh reminder that she planned to return to Boston, and he shouldn't forget it. Studying her, he wished he could know what she was thinking, what she was feeling as she fidgeted. His every gut instinct said she wanted him to kiss her. Doing so would be so easy. What came afterward would be anything but. He needed to go home.

"Glad to be able to further your education." As much as he should just turn and go, instead, he leaned forward and pressed a kiss to the top of her head, breathing in the scent of her shampoo and feeling a tiny clump of dried paint scrap the corner of his lips. Pulling back, he gently picked the tiny paint chip from her hair. "Night, Lottie. Sweet dreams."

"I…" Her lower lip disappeared, then she nodded. "Night, Linc."

He took a few steps down the drive.

"Linc?" she called, sending his pulse racing.

"Hmm?" He turned. She stood exactly where she'd been, Maritime nosing into a nearby palmetto that her leash just allowed her to reach.

"Are you sure you don't want me to walk you back?" She shook her head as if rattling her senses into place. "I mean, drive you back? It wouldn't be any problem to run you there."

Was her invitation innocent or an offer of so much more? His heart squeezed; he suspected it was a confused mix of both. "Go inside, Lottie. You need to rest up for whatever Jackie throws at you tomorrow." And he needed the walk home to help clear his head, then he'd clean up the paint mess they'd made in his bathroom. "Go. I'll wait until you're inside."

She hesitated, then nodded. Maritime in tow, she climbed the stairway leading to Jackie's porch. When the house light came on, he saw her silhouette linger, then close the door to disappear inside the house.

Taking a deep breath, Linc crammed his hands into his shorts pocket and took off toward his place in an emotionally tangled mess. With him living on the island and her grandmother being here, running into Lottie had been inevitable. He'd known that. What he hadn't counted on was just how much he'd still want her, how much he'd like the quick wit beneath the Boston exterior of the woman she'd become.

If anything, Lottie attracted him more than she had the summer they'd met.

That was saying a lot.

CHAPTER SIX

THE FOLLOWING DAY, Linc had barely arrived at Jackie's when Mrs. Baker walked over with Maritime's leash secured to the handle of a wagon she pulled over the sandy lawn.

"I spoke with Jackie just a little while ago. They were on Huntington Island so they should be here soon." She gestured toward the wagon. "I baked a few things to welcome her home. There's plenty of those cookies you love in there, too, so be sure to help yourself. While I'm thinking of it, thanks again for unclogging my drain last week."

"No problem on the drain." Linc's mouth watered at the thought of Mrs. Baker's chocolate no-bake cookies. "You trying to fatten me up, Mary?"

The older woman laughed but was saved from answering by Lottie turning the car into the driveway and clicking open the door to the basement garage. From the back seat, Jackie waved as they passed. Maritime went crazy barking and bouncing around to where she freed her leash from the wagon handle. Barking, she charged toward the car that had just parked and excitedly jumped up to peer in at Jackie. *Bark. Bark. Bark.*

Linc and Mrs. Baker took off after the dog, attempting to keep her from scratching the car's paint. Jackie was now talking to the dog, so Maritime wasn't having being pulled away from her favorite person whom she hadn't seen in days.

Bark. Bark. Bark.

"Maritime, shush! Would it have been easier if I hadn't pulled the car into the garage?" Lottie spoke loudly to be heard over the dog. Perhaps giving up, she opened the car's back door. The dog jumped in, licking Gram's face in an excited welcome home. Laughing, Gram loved on the dog. "Don't let her bump your foot," Lottie reminded her, then glanced back at Linc. "I wasn't really thinking about which set of stairs would be easiest to get Gram up. Is this even going to work? I should have hired someone to help you get her inside."

Linc eyed her, wondering at her nervousness and finally attributing it to Gram's coming home. "She barely weights a hundred pounds soaking wet. I don't foresee getting her inside the house as being a problem, do you?"

Lottie's gaze dropped to his arms. Her throat worked. "Uh…no, I guess not so long as I can keep Maritime out from under your feet."

"Hello, I am right here, you two," Jackie said from the car's back seat. "It's my foot that's broken, not my hearing."

Lottie shot her grandmother a look. "Getting you into the house would be a lot easier if it was your hearing."

Linc laughed. "Lottie has a point, Jackie. You sure went to a lot of effort to get me to carry you across your threshold."

Her arms around Maritime's neck as she hugged the dog to her, scratching behind her ears and managing to keep Maritime from licking her face, Jackie snorted. "If I'd wanted you to carry me across my threshold, you'd have done so long ago."

Linc chuckled again. "I imagine I would. You Dunlap ladies are hard to resist."

"I wouldn't go as far as to say that," Lottie mumbled. Linc wasn't sure if Jackie heard over Maritime's excited whimpers and barks, but he had. Did Lottie think his walking away the night before had been easy? Far from it. Under the circumstances, the best thing he could do was resist anything other than her friendship.

"Wrap your arms around my neck, Jackie." He squatted beside the car. "Once you've gotten hold, I'll slide you toward me, then put my arm beneath your legs to support you as I lift you from the car."

"Maybe it's you who has been wanting an excuse to have my arms around you," Jackie accused, doing as he told her and doing a decent job of hiding any pain. Other than having to convince Maritime to move out of his way, he had zero problems scooping up Jackie.

"Get back, Maritime," Lottie ordered, pulling on the dog's leash in an attempt to hold her back. "You're going to trip Linc and hurt Gram."

"She's fine," he assured her, being careful not to let the dog's jumping knock him off-balance or hit Jackie's injured foot.

Lottie followed behind him, fretting as if she worried that he was going to hurt himself. He didn't make a habit of carrying patients, but Jackie didn't weigh much. His biggest concern was making sure the transfer into the house caused her the least amount of pain possible and that Maritime truly didn't trip him up.

"My little girl has missed me, hasn't she?" Jackie crooned, baby-talking to the dog from Linc's arms. "Just a little, haven't you, sweetie? And no wonder, you look as if you've lost weight. Hasn't Lottie been feeding you?"

"Nope," Lottie answered from where she and Mrs. Baker had followed them into the house. Lottie carried a folded lightweight wheelchair, and Mrs. Baker held a bag of Jackie's things. "Only good dogs get fed and that's not what she is."

Linc snorted. He suspected she'd overfed the dog, if anything.

"My Mari is always a good girl, aren't you?" Gram reached down to scratch the excited dog's head. "Linc, have you let Lottie starve my poor baby?"

"I tried to sneak her food, but you know what a stickler Lottie is for rules." Taking care to be gentle with her foot, Linc lowered Jackie onto the living room sofa.

Looking up from where she positioned Jackie's foot on a pillow, Lottie wrinkled her nose. "Your bad dog hasn't missed a meal."

"Maritime is not a bad dog."

"She's not good. Maritime," Lottie said in a strict voice. "Sit."

Four sets of human eyes looked toward the dog. As if to prove how wrong Lottie was, Maritime sat, stared up at Jackie with adoring eyes, and, tongue flopped out of her mouth, panted patiently while waiting for further instruction.

Linc tried not to laugh as Lottie rolled her eyes. "Of course, she listens when you three are

here, but normally, she ignores everything I say.
I've even tried treats to get her to listen, and they
haven't worked."

"Has she been mean to you?" Jackie asked
the dog, motioning for Maritime to come closer.
Maritime sniffed at Jackie's bandaged foot. "She
knows."

"I imagine she does. She's a smart girl." Linc
watched as the dog gently rubbed her nose
against the injured foot. "Maybe it'll make her
careful not to bump you. We can't have you falling again. Let's practice transferring from the
sofa to your wheelchair."

"Maybe later, when I've rested from the drive
home."

Linc shook his head. "I'm not leaving until
you show me that you can transfer from the sofa
to your wheelchair."

"While they do that, how about you and I
carry up the goodies I made? They're out in the
wagon," Mrs. Baker suggested, placing her hand
on Lottie's arm. With one last warning glance
toward her grandmother, Lottie followed Mrs.
Baker back outdoors.

Turning back to Jackie, he eyed her. "You
wanted to come home, which means you're
going to have to transfer yourself. Lottie can't
do it for you."

"You can just stay. There's another bedroom."

"Not happening." For so many reasons. "My staying wouldn't help you to get stronger."

"I'm plenty strong. My problem is that I can't bear weight."

"Which doesn't mean you can't transfer yourself so Lottie doesn't hurt herself trying to move you."

"You ever heard of hopping one-footed? I got this."

Linc stayed close to catch her if she wasn't as strong as she thought. "Fine. Prove it."

Just as he suspected, Jackie struggled to get into the wheelchair. "You tricked me, asking me to do that when I've had a long day and Maritime wants nothing more than to snuggle. Go help Lottie and Mary carry up the goodies. I'll have more strength after I've eaten."

Recognizing that he had gotten as far with the woman who'd leaned back against the sofa as he was going to get for the moment, Linc headed outside.

He was surprised that Lottie and Mary hadn't been back inside long ago. When he stepped outside on the porch, he grinned at the posse of neighbors who now stood in the driveway, each one carrying a dish. No wonder they hadn't made it back. Lottie must have used brute force to have kept them at bay this long, probably insisting that they couldn't interrupt Jackie's transfer.

"Oh, here's Linc now," Mary said, spotting him. "The ladies are here. Can we see her?"

"Sure thing."

Mary and the other ladies headed up the stairs to visit with Jackie, leaving Linc and Lottie on the lawn.

"Thank you for bringing Gram into the house and working with her when I know she doesn't make things easy."

"Not a problem. She's one of my favorite people in the world."

She gave him an odd look. "You mean that, don't you?"

"Why wouldn't I? She's feisty, but that's one of the things I most love about her." He gestured toward the house. "They'll be here a while so if there's anything you need to do, now would be a good time."

Worry clouded Lottie's eyes. "Tell me what to do so I can help her, Linc. I feel inadequate at being alone with her like this."

"You'll be fine." Linc gave her an empathetic look. He considered staying, but suspected Jackie would have him lifting her each time rather than putting in the effort to transfer herself. Sometimes need was the best facilitator. "She'll tell you what she wants you to do without hesitation, and you've made her extremely happy by doing what was necessary so she can recover at home. She missed her house and Maritime. I'll call to check on her later. If you need me, call. I'm only a few minutes away."

He took off down the drive. When he reached the road, he turned, caught her still watching and waved.

Smiling, she waved back and Linc was tempted to toss his plans so that he could spend the day with Lottie, helping her with Jackie and reassuring her that she had this. She did but he understood her doubts. Seeing a loved one not up to par was never easy, but especially not when it was someone as vivacious as Jackie.

He called that evening to see if she needed help putting Jackie to bed.

"It wasn't easy, but Gram and I got her into her wheelchair, to the bathroom and back to the sofa a few times. The last time she preferred to go to bed, and she was out within seconds."

Disappointment hit that he wouldn't be seeing her again. Maybe he should have stayed earlier, but… "This is the most active she's been in several days. Hopefully, she'll sleep through the night."

"Hopefully." Lottie yawned. "I straightened things up a bit and plan to call it an early night, too."

As if to emphasize her plans, she yawned again. Had taking care of Jackie worn her out or had she not slept well the night before? That he could relate to. He'd lain in bed for what seemed like hours, thinking over their painting fun and how much he'd wanted to kiss her, marveling at how the grown-up Lottie had looked at him.

"Get some rest, Lottie." If he didn't get his thoughts in check, he wouldn't be getting any sleep tonight, either. As restless as he felt, he'd probably work late into the night. "I'll be by in the morning for Jackie's therapy."

"Thanks. We'll be here."

Linc hung up the phone, then stared at it as a crazy thought occurred.

He had called…but twelve years too late.

Early the following morning, Jackie frowned at the equipment Linc carried into her living room as she reclined on the sofa. A neon-green-and-aqua pillow propped up her injured foot, and Lottie had styled her sandy-blond-gray hair into a long braid and dressed her in a loose T-shirt and pair of baggy shorts that would have easily gone over her cast.

"What's that?"

"Part of your therapy. Lottie gave me permission to rearrange things however I needed to for your sessions." Placing the folded rowing machine onto the tiled floor, he repositioned a chair.

"Did she now?" Jackie eyed him "I thought I had to be non-weight-bearing."

"Sitting is non-weight-bearing," he assured her, opening the rowing machine. It wasn't the fanciest model but would work great for what Jackie needed.

"You need to maintain good blood flow and to keep your muscles from atrophying. Rowing is a good option as you get cardio, prevent muscle wasting, plus strengthen your core to help with balance and posture. We'll start with just doing upper body and will progress to adding your good leg, then on to using both legs when cleared to do so by Dr. Collins."

Jackie's forehead wrinkled. "You're supposed to help me walk again, not train for the Olympics."

Linc grinned. "I don't think they have a category for sassy old lady, or you'd be a shoo-in for gold."

"Lifetime of training," Jackie agreed, practically giggling even though she still eyed the machine with doubt.

"Are there one-pound weights around here?" Linc glanced toward where Lottie stood at the edge of the living room, the hand over her mouth no doubt trying to smother a snicker.

"None that I know of." Lottie looked at her grandmother for verification.

Jackie snorted. "Do I look like the kind of person who prances around her house in leotards, leg warmers, and weights in her hands?"

Linc chuckled.

"I can ask Mrs. Baker to sit with Gram so I can run into Beaufort to purchase some," Lottie offered.

Linc shook his head. "No need. We can improvise. Get me a couple vegetable cans."

Lottie went to the kitchen to grab the requested items.

He turned to Jackie. "You're going to stretch, then do weights. After that, we'll move on to the rowing machine."

Jackie crinkled her nose. "When all that work takes me nowhere, that's just useless."

"It's not only not useless, but necessary if you want to get well without setbacks."

"I suppose." Jackie's gaze went beyond him to the window-lined back wall. There was a screened porch to the other side, but the view of the canal was still excellent. "Being cooped up indoors is enough of a life setback."

Linc's heart squeezed at the longing on her face. "How about we make a deal? You do all your therapy with good effort, and I'll put you on the swing beneath your oak tree."

Jackie's face brightened. "You have a deal. I'm going to go crazy if I don't get outdoors soon."

As someone who rarely spent her waking hours indoors, he imagined Jackie was going stir-crazy after her hospital stay.

Lottie returned with a can in each hand. "Look what I found. Sixteen ounces each. Woot-woot."

Jackie cocked a brow. "Where's yours?"

Lottie placed the cans on the end table nearest her grandmother. "I'm not the one in therapy."

"Nope, but most things are easier if you have someone doing them with you and cheering you on." Jackie's expression was expectant.

"I'll be cheering you on." Linc was torn. Part of him wanted Lottie there, to experience her smiles and laughter and have them brighten his day, but another registered that if she stayed, he'd have trouble keeping his mind on Jackie.

"You planning to get out your pom-poms?" A smile played at Lottie's lips. "I can see you now. Go, Gram. Go, Gram. Go—"

Jackie chuckled. "That would be a sight. Our Linc shaking pom-poms and doing cartwheels."

"No pom-poms, but I can do a cartwheel." He paused. "Well, I could do a cartwheel. I honestly haven't attempted one in years but imagine I still can."

"That's what we all tell ourselves and then one day, we can't do the things we once could." Jackie turned pleading eyes toward Lottie. "Stay. Having you here makes me feel better."

Linc had no doubt that Jackie could do the exercises he had planned for her, but the look she gave Lottie was a humdinger.

"Then I'll stay. I'll go grab some cans for me, too."

"You're a spoiled woman, Jackie." Linc scrolled through his music playlists, chose a motivational one, then grinned. "Did I say spoiled? I meant soon to be sweaty."

"A little sweat never hurt anyone." Jackie picked up her cans. "Tell me what you want me to do so I can go outside. There's an ocean breeze with my name on it."

"I love your enthusiasm, but you need to stretch and warm up prior to going to the cans. We'll be doing similar things as we did during your session at the hospital. Put down the cans and hold your arms directly out like this." Jackie did as he instructed, following each stretching motion. "Now, I want you to make circles. Small ones at first, and then slowly work your way out to where you're doing bigger and bigger circles."

Linc ran through the exercises, having her rotate her arms, do an overhead triceps stretch and a cross-body stretch. Softly singing along with some of the catchy upbeat songs, Lottie did each of the exercises, too. Linc caught her gaze and, without thought, winked. Her gaze stayed locked with his for what seemed a long time but couldn't have been more than a few seconds. Seeming unsure what to do, she looked toward Jackie and thrust her arms back and forth into the air.

"Go, Gram. Go, Gram. You got this."

Smiling, Jackie eyed her granddaughter. "You seem happy."

"Hey, you were the one who said you needed me to cheer you on," Lottie reminded her, still waving her hands around and shaking her hips. "This is me cheering you on. Whoop. Whoop."

"Now, with the cans, do biceps curls. We'll do five sets of five with palm facing upward." There. Linc sounded professional. Rather than like the silly schoolboy he felt with Lottie bouncing around the living room. "When we're finished, then you'll rotate your wrists to where your palms face inward and repeat the five sets of five. After that, we're going to do the same with Arnold presses. That's where you bring your arms in at ninety-degree angles, then up and out. Five sets of five there, too."

Without a word of protest, a testament to how much she wanted him to carry her outdoors, Jackie pumped her arms in a quick, jerky manner.

"Slow. Steady. With purposeful movements," he said, demonstrating what he meant. Lottie followed suit, raising and lowering her vegetable cans. "Good job, Lottie."

"Teacher's pet," Jackie accused, looking amused.

Lottie arched her brow. "What does that make you, Gram? The class troublemaker?"

Laughing, Jackie slowed her pace, controlling each motion.

Barely into the third set, Linc noted that her arms were shaking. His goal wasn't to exhaust her muscles. Not today. So, he slowed her, having her take ten to fifteen second breaks between her sets of five. She finished the sets, but her arms were a little wobbly at the end.

"Good job. You, too, Lottie," he teased. No wobbly arms there. "Uh, next, we're going to do leg stretches. All non-weight-bearing, of course."

"Of course," Jackie repeated, mimicking him, her gaze going back and forth between them. Was it obvious how Lottie being there affected him? Was Lottie just as aware? Probably. His voice had crackled during that last set of instructions, and then there had been that wink.

"Can you stretch out your injured leg or does it feel too heavy with the cast?"

Jackie lifted her leg a few inches. "It's not light."

"So, on the next exercises I'll leave it up to you as to whether you do them with just your good leg or with both. I want you to stretch out your legs in front of you and just raise them, then lower them. If you can, do ten together, then ten with each leg. If you have any discomfort on the fractured side, then just work your good side."

Jackie lifted her leg off the sofa, then lowered it back. She kept her movements small but controlled.

"Excellent." Linc glanced toward where Lottie had sat down and was following suit. "You, too, Lottie."

"Thanks. This is a good warm-up for my run later."

Had a more dazzling smile ever existed? Or eyes so green?

He cleared his throat. "Stretching and warming up is always a good idea."

Not missing a beat, Gram suggested, "You should go run with Lottie, Linc. Refamiliarize her with the island. Can't have her getting lost."

"Seriously, Gram? I was here at Christmas."

Jackie pretended to be fully focused on her leg movements. "Lots of changes since then. I mean, Linc didn't even live here at Christmas."

"She has a point," he agreed. "The island has changed a lot." They both knew it wasn't true. Yes, older homes were occasionally replaced with newer structures, but his giving the Mc-Mahon place a fresh coat of paint and updated landscaping might be the biggest change since her last visit. "I can go for a run with you. Or I can visit with Jackie while you go. Either way."

"I don't want Gram left alone." At her grand-mother's eye roll, she continued, "Not yet, any-way."

"Rather than order those weights, you should see about getting a GramCam."

Lottie's gaze cut to him. "A what?"

"New parents call them baby monitors," he stage-whispered.

"I heard that," Jackie grumbled, shaking her head. "A GramCam—that's all I need. Y'all spy-ing on me."

"I was thinking of starting an online channel with you as the star," Lottie teased, pulling her phone out. "Gram TV, it could catch on."

Pulling his gaze from where Lottie typed something into her phone, Linc chuckled. "That was your last set of those, Jackie. Now, I want you to make small circles."

"More circles?"

"Yep. Only this time, with your legs. Small circles with your legs going toward your center to begin with. Let's do ten and then do ten with your legs going in an outward motion. Do your good leg first, then the other, stopping if the movement triggers pain."

They went through the rest of the exercises, all but the rowing machine and he'd planned to play that one by ear based on how quickly Jackie tired out, anyway.

"No rowing today," he announced.

Jackie looked relieved that he wasn't pushing her to do so. Although she was an active lady, she had spent several days in bed. It didn't take long for that inactivity to take its toll on one's strength and energy.

Expression turning suspicious, Jackie asked, "I still get to go outdoors?"

"Yep. You earned it." Linc folded the row machine and moved it against a wall so it wouldn't be in the way. "I'll check to make sure the swing is ready and then come back to carry you out."

"Best thing you've said all day."

Enjoying the early stages of the sunrise-streaked sky as she jogged along the street, Lottie pulled her cell phone from her waistband phone pocket and, slowing to a walk much to Maritime's displeasure, clicked it on. Gram, still sleeping peacefully in her bed, appeared on the screen. Lottie smiled. Ordering the GramCam Linc had suggested earlier that week had been a brilliant purchase and provided more freedom without worrying that Gram was awake and waiting for help to transfer from the bed to her wheelchair. Or worse, that Gram was doing so on her own to where she might fall. So far, she'd played by the "rules," but Lottie didn't expect that to last.

"Hey, you!"

Maritime barked and did a happy wiggle and tug toward where Linc leaned against his porch railing. Had Lottie subconsciously on purpose slowed in front of his place?

"Hey, you, back," she called, sliding the phone into her pocket. "Good morning."

He'd been so good with Gram that she couldn't help but appreciate him. That was why she was smiling, right? Because of how patient and kind he was to Gram? How he kept both Gram, and Lottie, smiling during the sessions Gram insisted Lottie do each day, too? Not that Lottie minded. She looked forward to seeing Linc work his magic on her grandmother. From the changes he'd already made inside his house, she knew he'd been good at his construction job, but for him not to have gone to PT school would have been a shame. He was an excellent therapist. Then again, as far as she knew there wasn't much he wasn't good at except long-distance relationships and returning heartbroken phone calls.

Linc hurried down the steps and as he drew nearer, Lottie forced her gaze to remain on his face rather than gawk at his impressive physique. He must have just finished working out as the edges of his hair were damp and, in places, his T-shirt clung to his chest.

He fell into step beside her. "Jackie still sleeping?"

She nodded. "Thanks for the GramCam suggestion and helping me set it up yesterday. It works like a charm. I feel better sneaking out this morning knowing I can see if she's awake."

"How'd she do last night? Has adding the rowing machine made her sore?"

"Not that she's mentioned. She was sleeping well when I just checked on her." There. That let him know why she'd slowed. "I appreciate everything you're doing for her, Linc. I know she's happier being at home and thanks to you, it's going better than I'd imagined."

Although Gram would never admit it, Lottie suspected she looked forward to Linc's arrival almost as much as Lottie did.

"You're the one who made that possible, by staying. If I wasn't here, you'd have hired a home health company or just driven her back and forth to Beaufort." Linc pointed toward a neighbor's yard.

Glancing that way, Lottie grasped Maritime's leash tighter, grateful the dog was more interested in something up ahead of them. She smiled at the buck, three does and fawn grazing there. The deer, smaller than mainland deer, were plentiful around the island, and Lottie and Gram had watched them playing numerous times as they fed and cut through Gram's backyard.

"If I could get her up and down the stairs so she could spend more time outdoors, she and I would both be happier. Maybe I need to convince her to have a lift installed."

"I don't mind helping you get her up and down them as often as you need me to. She'll be running circles before they could have it built, but having a lift isn't a bad idea if Jackie can afford it." He offered to take Maritime's leash and Lottie handed it over. So far, the dog had been fairly well behaved but that could change any moment.

"Gram's artwork is quite successful, but even if it wasn't, money isn't an issue. My grandfather left her well provided for." A car pulled onto the road, and they moved to the shoulder.

Kneeling to hold Maritime's collar to prevent the dog from possibly taking off after the car, Linc waved at the couple as the car passed. "That's good. One less thing to worry about.

You never talked much about your grandfather, just mentioned that he died from a heart attack."

Resuming their walk, Lottie brushed some hair that had come loose from her ponytail back from her face. "He died when I was too young to remember much. He was the glue that kept my mother and Gram civil." Her heart clenched at the thought of her mother, and she was struck with the same deep grief of missing her that always hit. "When Gramps died, Mom didn't come back to the island until the summer I was here, and Gram quit leaving."

She'd never understood the animosity between her mother and Gram, and neither had been able to give her a reasonable explanation. Lottie had always thought they'd someday get along, that maybe she'd be able to facilitate that. With her mother's passing, that had never happened and never would. How her mama could have been such a devoted and loving mother and yet a mostly estranged daughter to Gram had always boggled Lottie.

"I'm sorry. I recall you mentioning that he's why you wanted to be a cardiologist. You said you wanted to be a heart doctor so you could prevent as many other kids as possible from losing their grandfather the way you'd lost yours."

Lottie glanced toward him. He remembered that? "We were lying on the beach, listening to the waves and each other's life ramblings when I told you about Gramps dying. You always listened to my ramblings as if I was spouting something brilliant."

"In my eyes, you were."

Warmth spread through Lottie's chest. "I think the same about you."

"There wasn't much brilliant about the kid I was back then, but I was impressed at how you knew exactly where you were going in life. That you'd applied to Harvard and, not just gotten accepted, but also landed a prestigious scholarship."

Embarrassed at his praise, Lottie shrugged. "I'm still not sure how that happened."

"I am. You deserved it. I never doubted that you'd become an amazing cardiologist."

"For all you know I could be an awful cardiologist," she teased to offset the warmth filling her at his praise.

He shook his head. "Even if I hadn't seen how great you were with Mrs. Stephenson, I know better."

"How is she doing?"

"Great. She's scheduled to resume her knee rehab next week."

They reached the beach area, but rather than turning to head back, Lottie crossed through the opening in the large rocks to head toward the water. "Do you mind? The sunsets are beautiful, but don't compare to the sunrises. I've always loved coming here to watch them, but this is the first morning I've ventured out to experience one."

"This is your run, although not as much of one since I interrupted and likely made you miss a good portion of the sunrise. Sorry about that."

The half-mast sun painted the horizon with orange, red and blue streaks. "Don't be. I'm enjoying your company."

He glanced toward her and grinned. "Ditto."

The word he'd used so often in the past, especially when she'd said I love you, had Lottie's breath catching. To hide her reaction, she bent to take off her shoes to keep out the sand and let the waves lap at her feet. "Who would have ever thought we'd be friends?"

First unhooking Maritime's leash to let the dog take off across the empty beach, Linc bent to take his shoes off, too. "It's not that odd. We were on the best of terms when we said our goodbyes."

"You're right. We were."

They'd been on this very beach, sitting on a blanket and watching the sun go down.

"This summer has been the best of my life," Lottie said, stealing a glance at Linc. *"I can't believe it's over, that I'll be leaving tomorrow."*

Linc squeezed her hand. "It has been a great summer."

"So great you don't want to continue our relationship, though?" she prompted, still not quite wrapping her brain around the idea that tonight was really the last time she'd ever see him.

He loved her. She knew he did. It was in the way he looked at her, smiled at her, touched her as if she were the most precious thing he'd ever know. According to him, she was.

"We've talked about this, Lottie. We end now." He swallowed, though, as if he wasn't quite as sure as he claimed. "You're going to be busy with school. I'm going to be busy with school and work. We'd try to squeeze each other in, managing a few holiday visits at first, but ultimately we'd become disillusioned, holding each other back until one of us called it quits, and we'd never view this summer the same. Don't you think it would be better to keep our memories of each other perfect?"

"I guess."

What he said made sense on the surface. Having a thousand miles between them wasn't going to be easy. But Lottie didn't buy that they'd be better off completely severing all ties. Nor did she buy that he wouldn't change his mind.

She knew he missed her on the rare occasions they'd gone twenty-four hours without see-

ing each other. A few weeks apart and he'd see that she was right, that although it wouldn't be easy, their love was stronger than any distance or busy schedule. They'd make it work.

Confident in the knowledge that Linc loved her, Lottie leaned over and kissed him.

They'd have their dreams and each other, too...

Memories of that evening, that night, squeezed Lottie's heart, making breathing hard, so she stepped into the inlet's cold water, hoping it would jar her system. How naive she'd been. He'd meant his goodbyes and she'd been the one missing him like crazy, almost throwing her dreams away to chase after him. Walking out until the water was knee-high, she stared across Skull Inlet toward Pritchard's Island where an abandoned University of South Carolina research lab had once stood. It had now been demolished, erasing yet another piece of her beloved Fripp memories.

"You used to run out into the water, arms wide and your face turned up to the sun," Linc said from behind her. "That girl was my best friend."

"For a single summer," she said low enough she doubted he'd hear over Maritime splashing where the dog had followed her into the water. She and Linc had been inseparable, and she'd been young enough not to let what would happen at summer's end prevent her from loving him with all her heart. She'd never been that trusting, that naive, again.

Sighing, she turned to see Linc standing just behind her.

His gaze met hers. "It was a great summer, Lottie."

The best.

Everything that had happened since didn't change the magic she'd felt with him. And maybe that's exactly what he'd meant that day. Not that she agreed, but time had kept pressing forward and so had she.

He took her hand and, clasping it, brought it to his lips. "The best."

Had he read her mind?

Hand in hand, they walked back to the sandy beach while keeping an eye on where Maritime played. Rather than bend to pick up his shoes, Linc let go of her hand and surprised her by leaning forward in a stretching motion.

Curious, Lottie eyed him. "What are you doing?"

From his bent over position, he grinned. "Prepping myself."

"For?"

"You'll see." He put his hands above his head, swayed back and forth in another stretch. Then with a quick motion, he lowered his hands to the ground, rolled forward, and landed back on his feet. Sort of. "Ta-da."

Shaking her head at his silliness, Lottie laughed. "Don't hurt yourself."

Attempting another that was so poor that Lottie knew he wasn't even trying, he pretended to be offended. "Are you making fun of my cartwheel?"

She pretended surprise. "Is that what that was? I'm not saying it was bad, but it might be in the running for the worst cartwheel in history."

"Oh, really?" Grabbing her by the waist, he picked her up and carried her back out into the water. "Take it back, Charlotte Fairwell."

Maritime chased after them, barking and splashing through the water, leaping around as if she were part of their play.

"Or you're going to drop me?" Laughing and clinging to him so she could take him down with her if he did attempt to toss her, Lottie shook her head. Lord, he felt so good against her.

"There you go proving how smart you are again. Harvard would be proud."

Only Lottie wasn't sure she was smart, at all. A smart woman would let him drop her into the inlet, so his arms weren't wrapped around her body, so she wasn't pressed against a body she'd once known as intimately as her own. Or maybe a smart woman would hold on so tightly that he'd never let her go. If she had that goodbye to do over, that's what she'd do. Hold on with all her might, all her heart, to what they shared. Was it too late?

"Okay, okay," she said, giving in. "Since Maritime obviously isn't coming to my defense, I take it back."

"Why don't I believe you?"

"You told me to take it back." She stretched to try to reach the water so she could splash him, but her fingertips didn't quite make it. "You didn't say I had to mean it."

"Yep. Smartest girlfriend I've ever had." To her surprise, as she'd been prepared to be soaked, he lowered her to her feet to where the water was midthigh, dampening their shorts. Rather than dunk her, he even made sure she was steady on her feet and that Maritime didn't knock her over with her excited leaping.

Picking up a piece of driftwood, Linc tossed it toward the shoreline. Excited, Maritime took off in pursuit.

Walking beside him through the water, Lottie couldn't resist asking, "Have there been many?"

"Girlfriends?" Linc shrugged. "A few."

Which didn't tell her much and curiosity got the better of her.

"Any that stand out?"

"Just one."

Heart pounding, Lottie almost face-planted into the water. She didn't have to ask and he didn't have to confirm for her to know who he meant. He meant her.

"I didn't think I'd ever date someone after you," she admitted. "I didn't think it worth risking the pain of another heartache." Need to understand what had happened, to know if she'd been wrong about him, about them, overwhelmed her. "Why didn't you call me back, Linc?"

Jaw tight, he didn't say anything, just took the stick Maritime had retrieved and gave it another fling, then glanced at his watch. "We should head back. If she's not already, Jackie will be waking soon."

Seriously? He was going to ignore her question? Lottie wanted to tackle him, knock him into the water and splash him until he begged for mercy and told her everything she wanted to know. But he was right. Gram probably was awake. Guilt hit that she hadn't opened the GramCam app since he'd joined her in front of his house. She pulled out her phone, looked to see that Gram was indeed awake and reading the note Lottie had left her. "I need to get back."

To Gram's…and to reality.

CHAPTER SEVEN

"WHO WOULD HAVE thought a broken heel would be so much trouble?" Taking a break from the variety of seashells she glued to a piece of driftwood, Gram stared out at her backyard view of the canal. "I miss being on the water."

"You've barely been home a week," Lottie reminded her, sitting on the opposite side of the card table she and Linc had set next to Gram's swing so she could work. Linc had jogged back to Ole Bessie with her, saying that he would get Gram's therapy session done first thing. Otherwise, they'd barely said a word since her asking the question that had haunted her for twelve years.

Gram had cooperated fully thanks to Linc's promise to take her outdoors after her session. After getting her comfortable, he'd escaped Lottie's questioning, and perhaps accusatory, looks to his house with a request for Gram to call whenever she was ready to go indoors. Lottie suspected that might be never with the way Gram had settled into the swing and longingly eyed the occasional boats passing through the canal.

"That's too long."

Lottie imagined it was to Gram who spent time most days on the water, weather permitting. The large oak provided great shade, and a breeze blowing in from the ocean relieved the sticky warmth that Gram seemed impervious to as she semi-lay on the double swing. Lottie had placed a colorful pillow on the cushioned swing to keep Gram's foot elevated. Maritime dozed a few feet away. Keeping her grandmother busy and motivated was going to be the key to keeping her compliant and staying off her foot until the orthopedist released her to start using crutches.

"You'll be back on your feet in no time," Lottie said. "But having this injury happen does make me question you going out to Pritchard's by yourself so frequently."

Gram's expression turned saccharine. "Guess you'll just have to move home so you can keep an eye on me then."

Lottie's stomach clenched. "You know I can't do that. I have a contract with the hospital in Boston. Maybe you should move up north." Gram's expression grew horrified, and Lottie laughed. "You look as if I just suggested something sacrilegious."

"You did." Gram crossed her arms. "I was born in South Carolina, and I'll die here."

Lottie's throat tightened. "Let's not even talk about that."

"Actually, we should talk."

This time Lottie imagined she was the one with a horrified expression. "It probably feels as if you're dying because you're having to remain immobile, but you're going to be fine."

Gram snorted. "I don't mean dying from this blasted foot. I meant, in general, when I die. Eventually it's going to happen, although Lord willing not any time soon. I need to know that you won't sell this place after I'm gone." She reached out to pet Maritime who'd awakened, stretched, then moved next to the swing. "Nor do I want my Ole Bessie to rot from lack of use and love just because I wanted her to stay in the family."

Having seen the McMahon beach house, which she'd loved, deteriorate more and more with each visit, Lottie understood exactly what her grandmother meant. No doubt the entire island was cheering that Linc had bought the place.

"I can't move here, Gram." Not even if she wanted to, which she didn't. She loved being a cardiologist and taking care of her patients. She loved her life in Boston. Her coworkers and friends.

That Brian didn't immediately pop into her head as a reason to love her life in Boston wasn't lost on her. If she had wanted to return to Fripp permanently, would he have been enough to keep her in Boston? Would she have been willing to change the course of her life to be with him the way she once had with Linc? She adored him as a friend, but he wasn't enough. She knew it. Perhaps he did, too, and that's why he hadn't mentioned picking out a ring for so long. Yet, letting him go felt a betrayal to her parents, to her mother. Vivien had loved Lottie with all her heart and she'd thought Brian was perfect for her, so he must have been. And maybe, at the time they'd met, Brian had been because he'd never made demands of her, never held her heart strings to where he could yank on them at will. She'd never given him that power. Doing that would have been risking getting hurt again.

Oblivious to where Lottie's thoughts had gone, Gram gave Maritime another pat, then picked up a shell and studied the swirling center. "I plan to set up a trust to ensure you can keep the place spiffy so that you can bring my future great-grandchildren here and, hopefully, someday, they can bring their children."

Her children. Grandchildren. No matter how much she tried Lottie couldn't picture children who looked like her and Brian. Not even to honor her beloved mother's memory did she see that ever happening.

"You can teach them about the island and to have an appreciation for the South." Gram pulled Lottie's attention back. Good. Her previous thoughts would open a Pandora's box she knew better than to mess with, but realized she couldn't in good conscience ignore. Brian deserved better than that. And so did Lottie.

She watched the woman she loved so much twist and turn a wire around an end of the driftwood, then attach more shells. Lottie picked up a shell and began gluing it to her own piece of driftwood. They worked in silence until Gram was satisfied with her work and leaned back in the swing to eye Lottie's piece.

"You're pretty good."

"I just glued pieces where they fit."

Gram grinned. "Exactly."

Her genuine praise pleased Lottie and, taking a deep breath, she said, "Gram?"

"Hmm?" Gram looked up from where she'd been loving on Maritime.

"I'm not going to marry Brian."

* * *

"I know your grandmother doesn't like me, but I didn't think she'd convince you to end our relationship."

Lottie paced across the sunroom to stare out the window at where her grandmother still sat in the swing with Maritime by her side. Mrs. Baker and another neighbor visited with her, laughing at something Gram was saying.

"This isn't about Gram. It's about you and me, Brian. I adore you, but I'm not in love with you."

That doesn't matter, Lottie. You can learn to love him, her mother's voice whispered.

No, Mama. I can't. I won't.

"You're not in love with me either, Brian. Not really. Maybe you were once upon a time, but if you're honest, you're more in love with the idea of us as a couple than you are specifically with me."

"If I've done something to give you the impression that I don't love you, then you're mistaken."

"As a dear friend doesn't count," she pointed out, then sucked in a deep breath. "Not when that's all there is. When you've had time to think about what I'm saying, you're going to know I'm right."

Silence came over the phone for long moments. "It's him, isn't it?"

"Him?"

"The guy you were so torn up about when we first met. You told me that you weren't sure about our dating because you hadn't gotten over someone you'd once known. Your mother told me not to worry because she knew you and I were perfect together, but he's always been between us, hasn't he, Charlotte?"

Lottie squeezed the phone so tightly her fingers hurt. "Mama talked to you about Linc?"

"Just to say that she was happy I'd come into your life and brought a smile back to your face. That she'd known from the first moment she'd met me that I was the one to fill the void that had been in your life."

Guilt hit Lottie so hard she could barely breathe. "Your friendship did fill a void in my life. Yours and Camilla's. I love you both dearly. But I'm not willing to pretend that we're anything more than friends. Not anymore."

"I'm not sure what to say, Charlotte. I'm not even sure what you want me to say."

"That makes two of us," she admitted, trying to calm her shaking hands. "This is scary because you've been a part of my life for the past five years and what I thought my future looked like and now I just don't know."

Another pause, then, "I never wanted to be your safety net."

And yet that's exactly what he'd been. Safe, undemanding, unable to wreak the havoc upon her heart that Linc had, and she'd embraced that. Her mother had mistaken that and friendship for something more and because Lottie had wanted to believe, she'd let her mother convince her of the same.

"You deserve better," she said, and meant it. "I hope you find someone who loves you as you deserve to be loved, Brian."

Hanging up the phone, Lottie sank into the sunroom's oversize hanging chair and gave in to the tears streaming down her face.

Forgive me, Mama. I miss you so much, love and respect your opinions, but this is my life and I have to live it.

That evening, after they'd gotten Gram settled on the sofa, Lottie walked onto the front porch with Linc. As always, he'd been amazing with Gram. Part of her had wanted to immediately tell him that she had ended things with Brian, but after his reaction to her question that morning, she held back. Once she'd had her big boo-hoo fest, she'd cleaned her face and spent the remainder of the afternoon playing cards with Mrs. Baker and Gram.

"Thank you for taking such good care of Gram. She had a really good day today with getting to spend so much time outdoors, but I know this has to be slowing down your work on your house."

He shrugged. "Unless some helper mermaids come ashore and finish the job for me, it'll be waiting on me after Jackie is back on her feet. There's no rush."

"Helper mermaids, eh?" Lottie smiled. "Just because there's no rush doesn't make it right for us to take advantage of you, Linc."

"Neighbors helping neighbors isn't taking advantage." He leaned against the railing, staring out into Gram's yard. "Besides, I owe your grandmother. It's thanks to her that I got the McMahon place."

Lottie stared at him. "What do you mean?"

"She's never said anything, but Mrs. McMahon's son said she called and convinced him to take my offer over the others they received."

Gram had done that? Why would she care who bought the house?

He pushed off the railing. "I work tomorrow, but I'll stop on my way home and take her outside for an hour or so. It's not much, but short of getting her out there at the crack of dawn and her being stuck out there all day, it's better than nothing."

"It's wonderful and much appreciated. Thank

you." She bit into her lower lip. "Is there anything we can do for you?"

He shook his head. "I'm good."

Lottie agreed. Linc was good. Better than good.

Why wouldn't you answer my question? Would it be so difficult to just admit that you hadn't loved me the way I thought you did? The way I loved you?

"You're blushing, Lottie." Curiosity laced his voice.

"I got a little too much sun today when I was sitting outside with Gram." Because she didn't want to ruin the evening by telling him what she'd really been thinking. If she told him, he'd just change the subject or leave.

"You think?"

She knew.

True to his word Linc came by after he got off work the following day. Knowing she wanted to do something to show her gratitude for all he was doing for Gram, Lottie had left Gram playing cards with her friends long enough to make a grocery and shrimp boat run. The least she could do was cook dinner. She might have gone a bit overboard though, with steak, shrimp, pasta, rosemary potatoes and spinach salad with fresh fruit.

"Wow." Linc eyed the spread. "If this tastes half as good as it looks, then I'm going to need to spend some extra time working out in the morning."

Pleased by his reaction, she smiled. "Then let's hope you have to rise extra early."

He glanced around the cleaned kitchen. "What can I do to help?"

"Let's get Gram moved to either a lounger or the swing, whichever she prefers, and we can eat outside, if you're okay with that? She's been itching to go out all day."

"Will do."

Her grandmother had been sitting in the living room, watching a television program about couples getting married at first sight.

"Is this not just the craziest thing you've ever heard?" she asked as they came into the living room. Prior to the break, Lottie suspected her grandmother only had the television for her beloved weather station, but "reality" shows were helping fill her time resting on the sofa with her foot propped up. "People volunteering to marry someone they've never met and that a television producer has picked out?" She tsked. "You know this is just for theatrics and not real. Who would agree to something so ridiculous?"

"Maybe someone who has given up on more

conventional means of finding love," Lottie offered, half teasing.

"Actually," Linc said with a straight face, "I've been thinking about auditioning. You think they could find my soulmate?"

"No."

Two sets of curious eyes shifted to Lottie at her rather firm response.

"No?" Linc's brow lifted. "I'm that hopeless?"

Far from it. "I mean, there's better ways to find one's soulmate than some random person a Hollywood producer chose to boost ratings."

His blue eyes twinkled with a mixture of mischief and something more. "What would you suggest?"

Why was he teasing her about this? And in front of Gram!

"Take out a billboard with your photo on it." Gram practically cackled. "Women would line up."

Lottie couldn't argue. Linc was a handsome man, but there was so much more to him than his beautiful exterior. He genuinely cared about others, was intelligent and seemed to know how to do just about anything. His smile made a person feel good inside, an innate warmth and friendliness that just spread happiness. At least, that's how he affected Lottie.

Being around Linc did make her happy. Always had.

Linc chuckled. "I doubt that, but I imagine there would be a few takers when they saw my house. The McMahon place might be a real chick magnet."

"You'd have more than a few takers if you lived in a cardboard box," Gram assured him. "Tell him, Lottie."

"Way to put me on the hot seat there, Gram." Cheeks heating, Lottie glanced toward Linc. "I'm sure lots of women would jump at the chance if they knew you were looking."

Linc eyed her. "Would you? If you were single, I mean?"

Yes. No. She didn't know. Wasn't that what she'd been trying to figure out for the past twenty-four hours that she had been single? She was only there for a short time. Linc was her past, her present, but he likely wouldn't be her future outside of precious memories. Would a smart woman grasp at the chance to retaste the sweetness of the best summer of her life when she knew that warmth would only make the winter all the colder?

"I did," she reminded him, knowing she needed to give an answer. "When I was single."

I'm single now. She'd wanted to tell him the moment he'd walked into the house the night before, and it was on the tip of her tongue even now. But after thinking about little else for the past night and day, she hadn't fully processed just what her new relationship status meant. She hadn't even told Gram that she'd officially ended things with Brian. If she had, Gram would have been the one taking out a billboard—multiple billboards along Linc's drive to and from Beaufort and all advertising Lottie.

"That's right. You did." Linc's eyes darkened, momentarily losing their teasing gleam. "Maybe I'll put off my audition a little longer to give myself more time to work on the house, just in case I need a 'comes with an ocean view' tagline as a backup plan."

"If I was in my prime, you wouldn't need a backup plan." Gram gave Lottie a "you're crazy" look.

Chuckling, Linc scooped Gram up into his arms. "Just say the word, Jackie, and I'm yours."

Crazy! Gram's stare reiterated.

Opening the back door for them, Lottie followed the pair down the porch steps and readied the swing for her grandmother, making sure that the pillow was in the correct spot.

Gram was right. She was crazy. Crazy confused. Crazy guilty that she knew her mother was rolling over in her grave that Lottie had ended things with Brian. Crazy with the way her heart leaped when she was near the man who had yet again turned her life upside down.

As he got her grandmother settled, Lottie asked her, "How about I put a little of everything on your plate?" Lottie smiled at Gram's nod. She turned toward Linc. "Stay, rest and visit with Gram. Once I've taken care of her, I'll bring a plate for you, too."

"If it's all the same, I'll make my own."

"Yeah, yeah, leave me out here by myself," Gram mumbled, but didn't look as if she truly minded in the slightest.

"I think you just offended Maritime." Lottie gestured to where the dog had cocked her head.

"Come here, girl. You know I love you," Gram cooed to the dog as Lottie and Linc went into the house.

While he heaped generous portions of the food onto his plate, Lottie poured two glasses of lemonade and one sweet tea.

"This is amazing." Linc popped a potato chunk into his mouth. "When you texted to say not to eat anything as you were preparing dinner, I was prepared for pizza or burgers or something simple. If I'd known you could cook like this, I'd have suggested dinner long ago."

"What? And miss out on all the casseroles the neighborhood ladies have dropped by?" Lottie put her hands on her hips. "Besides, I can cook."

His eyes twinkled. "You couldn't when I knew you."

"I could. I just didn't," she said. "Mama and I had taken cooking lessons. She thought it was something fun for us to do together." Oh, how her teenage self had hated those weekly classes. Now she'd do anything to have those moments with her mother back.

I'm sorry, Mama.

Whether she apologized for not appreciating that precious time with her mother or that she silenced her voice as it started to beg her to re-think the security of her relationship with Brian, Lottie wasn't sure. "For a long time, cooking felt like a chore. At some point during residency, I realized cooking relaxed me and as a bonus I had really good leftovers to eat for the next week."

Glancing down at his full plate, Linc gave a sheepish grin. "I may have blown that 'leftovers for a week' plan."

Lottie shook her head. "If you're okay with it, I thought I'd cook dinner each evening you work and feed you for helping with Gram."

His smile slipped. "Lottie, you don't need to do that. I told you—"

"Please," she said, stopping him. "It gives me something to do to feel useful and Gram, too. I let her pick out the sides and dessert she wanted me to make. She even helped cut the potatoes."

He popped another potato into his mouth. "Well, if she's the one who picked these out, then I need to thank her. She must have thought I was going to be extra hungry."

"I invited Mrs. Baker to stay for dinner, too. She couldn't make it tonight but plans to come tomorrow."

"Lucky her. If word gets out on what an amazing cook you are, the whole island will be showing up for dinner." He set down his plate. "How about I carry out our drinks while you prepare Jackie's plate? I'll come back to bring mine and hers down while you get yours. That way you can join us sooner."

Handing the glasses over, she smiled. "Thanks. That sounds perfect."

They ate, laughed and enjoyed being outdoors, watching as several herds of deer passed. Maritime kept an eye on them, but otherwise ignored them.

When Linc got Gram back indoors and settled into her wheelchair where she'd asked to sit, he said, "I'll get out of you ladies' hair but I'm already looking forward to whatever you're making tomorrow evening. Tonight's dinner was delicious."

Happiness filled Lottie at his compliment.

He had eaten with gusto, as if he truly enjoyed every morsel, and she'd enjoyed watching him and Gram bicker over whether Emily Dickinson had been brilliant or off her rocker.

"Yes, dinner really was," Gram agreed. "Lottie's going to make a great wife someday."

"Don't go signing me up for your wedding reality show," Lottie warned, giving her grandmother a please-don't look. "I've no plans to marry anytime soon."

Although the mood was light, Linc's gaze bore into her. "Still no plans to go pick out an engagement ring, then?"

So much for wanting time to ponder her feelings, to sort her thoughts before sharing her news. This wasn't how she wanted to have this conversation. Not with her grandmother or with Linc. Was there even a reason to have it with Linc? But she didn't really see a way around answering him. Not unless she pulled one of his cues and just changed the subject. Tempting.

Instead, she took a deep breath and watched him closely to see how he'd react to her revelation.

"Brian and I are no longer a couple."

CHAPTER EIGHT

LOTTIE WAS SINGLE. Why hadn't she said anything earlier?

Just because she was single did not mean Linc had anything to do with that decision. Nor did it mean that if she was that he should feel so happy. He shouldn't. The pain in her voice when she'd asked why he hadn't called her back had almost undone him. Answering her would have hurt her worse than keeping his silence, so he'd kept his mouth shut. It's what he should do now. Lottie's time in South Carolina was as temporary as it had been the summer they met. In another few weeks Gram wouldn't need her there, and Lottie would return to Boston. She might even realize that she'd made a mistake in ending her relationship with the cardiologist.

"I'm not sure whether to say I'm sorry or congratulations," he said cautiously, doing his best to keep his voice level.

Jackie had no such reservations. "Definitely

congratulations. He wasn't the right man for her. Never was even if my granddaughter was too blind to realize that."

Lottie winced. "This turned awkward fast. Let's not talk about Brian."

Worked for Linc. He never wanted to mention the guy's name again.

"Are you sure you have to leave, Linc?" Jackie asked. "I need to keep my card game sharp, and Lottie's not a good player."

"Gram!" Lottie protested, causing Maritime to let loose with a yelp.

"What?" Jackie turned her hands up, then reached out to pet her dog. "You're not."

"No one's good at everything," Linc reminded her, eyeing the way Lottie's pulse pounded at her throat as if she'd just run to the beach and back. She might be acting as calm as he was, but she was just as on edge. "For the record, if I got to pick whether you could cook like an angel or cheat at cards like your grandmother, I'd pick the food every time."

Eyes searching his, Lottie sent him an appreciative smile. "Thank you."

"Hey," Jackie protested, as Linc had known she would. "I don't have to cheat at cards to win."

Pulling his gaze from Lottie's, he glanced toward Jackie. "Except for when you play me?"

"Does that mean that Linc beats you at cards?" Lottie sounded incredulous. "As in, when you don't have a partner to cause you to lose, he outplays you?"

Jackie frowned. "I wouldn't say he outplays me. He's just really lucky at getting the right cards."

"I beat her. Fair and square," Linc said, grinning. "Haven't you?"

"Rarely and only when she lets me so I'll agree to keep playing. Even then, I can tell she doesn't like it, but believes it a necessary evil because she loves to play so much."

Jackie blinked innocently, then clasped her hands together. "That settles it, Linc. You have to stay for at least one game so I can beat you both."

Linc's gaze met Lottie's, and he attempted to decipher what she wanted him to say. She lifted her shoulders in a slight shrug, but her eyes said, *stay*. "She'll trounce me if you go. Actually, she'll trounce me if you stay, but it would be worth it to see you take her down a peg."

"One game." There wasn't anything at home that couldn't wait. "But that's it. I'm a working man who has to be up early in the morning to work off my dinner."

Eyes still connected with his, Lottie smiled. "One game."

"One game is all it's going to take," Gram bragged. "I have a secret weapon tonight."

Linc pulled the coffee table over near the sofa while Lottie grabbed the card deck, paper and pen. "You think I'm going to let you win just because you have a cast?"

Jackie gave him a smug look. "Nope. Tonight, Lottie is my good luck charm."

"Rummy!" Lottie whooped, slapping her cards down on the table. "I win!"

"Let me see your cards." Jackie leaned forward, making sure Lottie's cards lined up as they should. Her voice had sounded brisk, but there was a light in her eyes that said Lottie's grandmother knew exactly how her granddaughter kept getting exactly the cards she needed and that she didn't mind nearly as much as her protesting would suggest.

Standing, Lottie moved to Jackie's side of the table and took her grandmother's hands, dancing around while holding them. "I want to hear you say the words."

Gram's lips twitched as she shook her head.

Laughing, Lottie happy danced all the more. "Come on, Gram. Say it. I beat you."

"And here I thought you'd be my good luck charm and instead that big oaf was yours."

Lottie's gaze cut to him, and he shrugged. "I

don't know what she's talking about. Congratulations on your win, though."

Lottie laced her fingers with her grandmother's and swayed them back and forth as if her grandmother joined her in her happy dance. "If Linc's why I won, then he's definitely staying for cards again tomorrow night."

Rolling her eyes, Jackie smiled. "You think you can beat me two nights in a row just because he's here? Doubtful, but I guess we'll see."

Linc moved the coffee table back to where it belonged, then told Jackie goodbye, grinning at her I-know-what-you-did look.

When he readied to leave, Linc wasn't surprised that Lottie walked outside with him.

"Thanks for staying." She followed him out the gate, taking care not to let out Maritime who'd come with them. "Gram and I had a great time tonight, especially me. Did you help me win?"

If she didn't know, he wasn't telling.

Linc latched the lock so Maritime couldn't push open the gate. "Jackie would have called me out if I was feeding your hand, surely?"

Lottie's eyes widened and he laughed.

"Linc! She'll get us both if she even suspects you helped me," Lottie accused, pushing against his arm.

Linc knew better. Jackie had enjoyed Lottie's smiles and laughter as much as Linc had.

"I play to win," he told her. As Jackie had suspected, he'd had difficulty concentrating with Lottie sitting across from him, smiling despite making bad play after bad play. He'd figured out real quick that beating Jackie might not happen but, unbeknownst to her, helping Lottie had been easy enough. Her delight had him feeling as if he had won.

She was still smiling and so was he. Not because of the card game, but because Lottie was single.

She laughed. "So you say, but now you have me wondering. You're a really nice guy, Linc Thomas."

"Uh-oh."

"What's that?"

"Nice guys never get the girl."

"No?" Breath audibly catching, smile faltering, she looked up at him. In the glow of the house's lights, her eyes glittered with uncertainty. "Does the nice guy want to get the girl?"

That one was a no-brainer, but he hesitated. There were so many reasons why he should let her down gently and go home before they made a big mistake.

"He does," he admitted, "but thinks getting the girl would complicate both of their lives, especially when the girl just ended a long-term relationship and might be confused about what it is she wants."

"I suppose you're right." She took a deep breath. "What do you want, Linc?"

You.

"Do you want to kiss me? Because in this moment, that's what I want."

Talk about complicating things. Lottie's question, how she was looking at him, sure did that. Or maybe it was how he answered that most complicated things.

Reaching out, he ran his fingers into her hair, letting the silky strands wrap around his hands as he pulled her close enough to inhale the citrusy scent of her shampoo. "I've wanted to kiss you from the moment I rounded the hallway corner and saw you standing there, soaking wet, and wrapped in a towel."

What he'd wanted was to strip off the towel and kiss her all over. He swallowed the lump forming in his throat and took a deep, steadying breath.

"You didn't say anything." Her response sounded accusatory.

"No," he agreed, lowering his hand. "You were bleeding, but more than that, you weren't single."

Lottie flattened her palms against his chest. "You're right, but Linc?"

"Hmm?"

"I'm single now." She stared up at him with such longing in her eyes that Linc couldn't breathe. If ever he'd heard an invitation to kiss a woman, that had been it. Only he couldn't. No matter how much he wanted to, he simply couldn't.

"So, you are." He drew upon every bit of will-power he'd ever had. Fingers still in her hair, he cradled her head in his palms and stared down into her lovely face. "I'm going home, Lottie, but not because I don't want to kiss you. Know that."

Disappointment shone on her face. That both pleased and tormented him.

"Mrs. Baker is sitting on her porch," he pointed out, in case she hadn't noticed her grandmother's neighbor watching them from the next house over. He wasn't sure there were binoculars involved, but light glinting off some-thing metal had been what clued him in to her presence. Part of him didn't care who saw, but having their first kiss in so long watched in that way bothered him.

"Oh!" Lottie took a guilty step back. "I, uh, yes, best not to kiss me when she'd tell Gram and that would have Gram thinking all kinds of things that just aren't the case." A nervous laugh escaped her throat. "She'd have us back together and be picking out names for our kids. What was I thinking? I never should have said anything about Brian and I not being together in front of her."

Her prattling had Linc's head spinning. She pressed her hands together and gave another of the laughs she made when nervous. That she was so obviously off-kilter put a huge dent in his willpower, but he managed to keep his feet in place and not close the distance she'd put between them.

"Perhaps not, but I am glad you said something in front of me."

Her eyes took on that wide-eyed uncertain look again. "You are?"

"You know I am, Lottie. I want to kiss you, to know if your mouth still tastes as sweet as honey and if the surf pounds my insides when you kiss me back. But I'm going to admit something else to you." Something he could barely believe himself. "I'm glad Mrs. Baker is there because as much as I want to kiss you, I'm not sure that I should."

Because he knew that all the reasons he shouldn't had nothing to do with her relationship with Boston Brian and everything to do with the fact that getting involved romantically with a woman destined to leave him yet again would be a big mistake on his part.

A big mistake he was destined to make.

Linc had worked the previous days but had stopped by each evening to take Gram outdoors, eat dinner with them and to play a single hand of cards, Mrs. Baker included. Each night, Lottie waited on him to say something, do something, that let her know he'd meant what he'd said, that he wanted to kiss her. He smiled. He laughed. He teased her. He made her smile and laugh and she teased him back. A crazy mixture of anxiety and anticipation was demolishing her insides.

After she'd practically thrown herself at him, she'd been prepared for awkwardness, but when he'd arrived the following evening, his warm smile, raves about his dinner and feeding her card hand to help her beat Gram in rummy had prevented that.

"Hey, Lottie, would it be okay to pack that up? Jackie has convinced me to go out on her boat to gather driftwood and whatever other treasure I run across. Mrs. Baker is going to come give her a few practice hands at winning cards." Gram grunted and Linc laughed. "How about it? Do you want to spend a few hours on the water with me? We can picnic on Pritchard's."

Just like old times.

Lottie nodded. "I— Sure. If Gram needs more supplies for her art, then we should definitely go see what we can find."

"Right. She needs the card practice, too. What with that three-night losing streak she has going."

"I'll remind you that your losing streak matches my own."

Lottie smiled. "Yeah, about that—"

"Lottie plans to make it four nights so be prepared for another defeat after we're back this evening," Linc warned. "I'll run home, grab my trunks and be back in say, thirty minutes?"

"Sounds perfect."

An afternoon alone with Linc. Yeah, that mixture of anxiety and anticipation was blowing full force, and as scary as she found not knowing what the future held, Lottie planned to run directly into the wind, face up to the sunshine for however long it lasted.

From the boat's front passenger seat, Lottie twisted to watch Linc drive. Once they'd exited the canal, rather than zooming straight across the bay to picnic at Pritchard's, Linc had headed into the inlet to drive through Gram's beloved marshes, pointing out birds and other wildlife.

"What a great surprise." Happiness flowed through Lottie. "It feels so good to be out of the house."

"Careful. You're sounding like Jackie," Linc teased, glancing toward Lottie. "You look a lot like her, you know. Or how she must have looked at your age."

Lottie nodded. She did resemble the photos she'd seen of Gram at her age. "I think it's the eyes." Lottie breathed in the sea air, relishing how doing so seemed to wash away every care. "As much as I'd love Gram to move to Boston, I'd never want to take away the joy she gets from coming out here. Not that Gram couldn't go out on the water there, too, but boating on the Charles River isn't the same as doing so in the South Carolina marshes."

Rather than answer, Linc just smiled and pointed toward the spartina grass to Lottie's right. He slowed the boat to a stop, cutting the engine a good distance from the tall green blades poking up from the water. There! A bottlenose dolphin broke the surface, then another, feeding, or maybe just playing at the grass's edge.

"Oh!" Excitement filled Lottie. Having grown up in Atlanta, her first dolphin sighting had been at the aquarium there during a field trip her mother had tried to talk her out of. Lottie's first wild sighting had been on Fripp with Linc when he'd pointed out a young calf swimming next to its mother. More than likely that calf, now grown, still lived in the area.

She looked toward him and was shocked to find him watching her rather than the dolphins. When their gazes met, he gave a lopsided grin that had her wondering if he was remembering how they'd watched for Bonnie and Baby Clyde, as they'd dubbed the mother and calf.

"They're still here."

Had he read her mind?

"Really?" She gazed at him in wonder. "You're sure? How do you know?"

"I've seen them. Bonnie has a new calf. According to the wildlife management agent I spoke with, she's had three since Baby Clyde."

"Three babies? I love that so much." Lottie turned her attention back to the dolphins, watching them play.

"I'd hoped we'd see them out here today."

"Oh!" she exclaimed when one came up a few feet from the boat. Reaching for her phone, she got her camera ready in case it came close again. After a few moments, two arched in unison, not as close as the one had been but midway between the boat and where they'd first spotted them. Lottie clicked away, hoping she'd gotten a few decent shots. Just as she was about to lower her camera, another surfaced close to the boat, perhaps the same one as before. He seemed to look right at her, smile, then duck back underwater. It surprised her so much that she hadn't clicked her camera a single time. Disappointment filled her that she failed to capture such a cool moment, especially since she'd had her phone in hand.

"Can you believe that?" She glanced toward Linc to see if he'd seen the dolphin. His phone was aimed her way. Realizing he'd been taking photos, hopefully catching the dolphin, she automatically smiled a cheesy smile. "Cheese."

Lowering his phone, he smiled. "I thought I got a great shot when your friend came up for a visit, but that one was better."

"Right." Lottie snorted. "I guess he just wanted to see what we were up to."

"Not sure if he's just curious about why there's someone else driving Gram's boat or if he's letting us know he knows we're here and eyeing his pod." Linc held one hand out to shade his phone's screen as he scrolled through the photos.

Lottie's attention wavered between him and the dolphins who continued to play as they moved farther along the grass edge.

"You'll like this one." Linc handed over his phone.

Lottie glanced down at the screen. He'd captured the dolphin looking at her and her excited profile as she looked back.

"Oh, Linc, will you send me this? I'd love a copy."

"Will do." He leaned toward her, placed his finger on the screen and scrolled the photo to the next one. "Keep looking."

Lottie's favorites were the ones with the dolphin, but the photos he'd clicked of her smiling at him weren't bad. Happiness shone on her face because she was happy. She dragged her finger across the screen again, excited to see the next shot, and paused. It was of her looking at him right before she'd said her cheesy "cheese." In her eyes she saw what she'd always known deep down. Even so, she wasn't willing to throw that label on what she was feeling. Her peace of mind wouldn't let her.

She lifted her gaze, found him watching her still. Did he see what was so obvious in that photo? "They're really good."

"Hard not to be with you in them."

Feeling way too breathy, Lottie handed his phone back, well aware of how their fingers brushed as she did so. How could she not be when that slight touch had sent electric tingles through her?

"Thank you. I think it's the fresh air and being away from working every day. I obviously needed a change of scenery more than I realized."

Linc slid his phone back into his shorts side pocket, zipping it to keep the phone secure.

"We'll go through the marshes for a while longer, then head to Pritchard's and picnic. Afterward, we'll see if we can come across some cool old boards or driftwood."

"Sounds perfect."

Watching him as he started the boat and guided them through the marshes, Lottie admitted that the entire day felt perfect.

Setting up the beach umbrella to provide shade on a good portion of the blanket, Linc stole a glance toward Lottie. She'd possessed an underlying cautiousness the past couple of days, but seemed completely relaxed that afternoon.

He understood her wariness. He felt the same. Part of him wanted to take her into his arms and kiss her until she was as breathless as just looking at her had him. Another part had told him to take things slow so he didn't muddle up either of their lives.

That he'd managed to keep away from the physical, knowing she was single and wanted him, was a testament to just how complicated things were and how he never wanted to hurt her again. He wouldn't. Even if it meant taking some things to his grave.

"Glad to see you enjoying yourself."

Lottie spread her arms. "What's not to enjoy about this gorgeous day?"

"True. We couldn't have asked for better weather."

"Nope." Lottie dug into the beach bag and pulled out plates, napkins, chips and a bag of cut up vegetables.

"Who knew a sandwich could taste this good?" Linc said, taking another bite.

"Agreed. I didn't realize how hungry I was." Lottie brushed crumbs from her lips with the napkin she kept tucked under her plate to keep the breeze from snatching it. "Thank you, Linc. This beats being at the hospital from dawn to dusk any day."

"Tell me about what you do," he requested, finishing off the last of his second sandwich and putting his utensils into the bag they'd brought with them.

Tentative at first, then with enthusiasm, Lottie told him about her work, the fabulous cardiologists she worked with and the innovative techniques for treating heart disease that they were developing. Hearing her passionate answer left no doubt about how much she loved her job.

They finished eating and sat watching the water, both the calmer inlet and the waves just beyond the barrier. Across the inlet, families had blankets spread, kids played in the water and several groups appeared to be playing Frisbee.

"Whatcha think, Lottie? You up for treasure

hunting? We can head over toward where they tore down the old research facility and look for items along the shoreline there. I doubt we'll find many shells—we'd have to come early for that—but there's usually some cool driftwood that way."

"There are cloth bags in the boat where Jackie puts things she finds." She'd taken him with her during her treasure hunts a few times. He'd gone, wanting to learn more about the islands, the water and about living on the island. She'd made him a housewarming gift out of some of their first trip's finds. He cherished the piece he'd hung on his bedroom wall.

After grabbing the bags from the boat, Linc and Lottie took off toward the east side of the barrier island. They covered the sandy shoreline and headed into a sparsely wooded area. Most of the trees along the shore were broken, and swayed from numerous storms that had battered the island over the years.

"Gram really has been busy this week and has turned out several new pieces. Well, you know that." Lottie laughed a bit nervously. "It's not as if she hasn't taken great pride in showing them to you when you've come by."

"She's very talented and so are you."

Cheeks turning pink, Lottie ignored his compliment of the piece she'd made. "Not everyone appreciates Gram's style, but I've always loved how she sees the world."

He stretched out his hand to assist her over a fallen tree. "Except when she's trying to interfere in your life?"

She climbed over the log, taking his hand to remain steady as she planted two feet back on the sandy ground. "You mean by sending us off together?"

"That would be one example," he agreed as they made their way through fallen tree debris.

"The latest example. I'm sorry she does that, Linc."

"It could be worse. She could not like me at all."

"She sure didn't like Brian and wasn't subtle about her feelings."

"She never is." He glanced her way, his gaze catching hers. "Regrets about your breakup?"

She shook her head. "Only that it should have happened long ago. We've really been more good friends than anything for way too long. It's what we started as and what we'll hopefully remain once he realizes we weren't right as a couple."

"What if he never realizes?" Had Linc? It had been twelve years and looking at Lottie, being near her again, seeing her smile, hearing her laugh, breathing in her goodness, had him wondering more and more what would happen if he gave in to how she made him feel. What if he gave in to the urge to taste her lips? Would the expected fireworks display instead be a few fizzled sparks? Or would he be so hooked that this time letting her go would be impossible?

If that were the case, then what? He'd heard how she talked about her life in Boston. Just this year he'd finally realized his dream of buying a house on Fripp. Long-distance relationships were hard. Wasn't that why they'd said their goodbyes at summer's end not expecting to someday have their reunion? He'd sure not expected Lottie to call him, begging him to change his mind and to call her. He'd believed when she got back to her reality, the sparkly shine of what they'd shared would dull and she'd realize circumstance had thrown them together and made everything seem so surreal. Recalling the raw emotion in her voice when she'd asked him why he hadn't called her back, he had to wonder if he'd been wrong.

"Hopefully, he will."

Could Linc? When whatever was going to happen between them prior to her returning to Boston, would he be able to just be her friend?

Linc glanced at where she walked next to him. Looking more beautiful than anyone had a right to, she pointed ahead.

"That's where the research lab used to be, isn't it?" Taking care with each step on the shifting sand, she headed toward where the dilapidated University of South Carolina research facility had once stood. "I still can't believe they tore it down. Every time a storm would come through, I'd ask Gram if it survived." She glanced toward him. "She refused to leave during the last big one. I was so worried. Promise me that, even if she's kicking and screaming in protest, you'll drag her off the island if there's another mandatory hurricane evacuation."

Everything Lottie said confirmed that she planned to leave, that staying wasn't an option.

"Why not ask me to promise something easier to keep like that I'll win the lottery or something? But you have to know that regardless of any promise I've made to you that I'd do my best to convince her to leave if I believed she was in danger."

"If only she saw danger the same as I did." She picked up a piece of driftwood. "I like this one."

He moved closer to inspect it. "Good eye."

"Thanks." She turned, smiled at him, and his heart thudded as their eyes met. The ocean sounds around them quieted. As the world stood still, her smile faded and her green gaze deepened. She sucked in a little breath that had

Linc's own breath feeling sketchy. His pulse beat as wildly at his throat as the waves pounding against the barrier that protected the inlet.

"Linc?" She pulled her lower lip between her teeth. His gaze dropped. He wanted to kiss her. To feel her lips against his. If he kissed Lottie, he was asking for heartache. He knew that. When he'd invited her out for the day, he'd known. Known they'd be alone, that this moment would come, this decision would have to be made. Never had he dreamed he'd hesitate and yet he couldn't quite close the gap between their lips. Did he really want to do this when he knew how it was going to end? When ultimately, she'd leave him again?

How her eyes had lit up when she'd been talking about her work had him taking a step back.

Don't do this to her. To yourself.

Lottie mustn't have had the same concerns, though. Or if she did, the sunshine had melted them away. She stretched onto her tiptoes and pressed her lips to his.

Fireworks, he thought. No fizzled-out sparks, but massive, light up his world, July Fourth fireworks.

CHAPTER NINE

"THE BOAT'S STILL THERE," Lottie said from where she walked next to Linc, treasures in hand. Had they not found so many excellent pieces of driftwood and even an old piece of a sign washed up from who knew where, Linc imagined they'd have held hands on their way back to the boat.

"Did you think it wouldn't be?" He chuckled. Then again, would he really have been surprised if Jackie had hired someone to take off in the boat, abandoning them on the island? Not that he couldn't have swum across the inlet to Fripp. He'd done it in the past when the tide was lower, but he wouldn't have allowed Lottie as the currents could be tricky and grab hold before one realized.

Physical attraction could be tricky and grab hold before one realized, too.

Lottie's kiss for example. Sweet and that of a siren all in one fantastic moment. He'd kissed her back. How could he not have when he'd tasted the vulnerability on her lips? Linc might have been the one who'd worried he hadn't measured up all those years ago, but Lottie felt emotionally exposed, as well.

If only it was just physical attraction. If that were the case, he'd have made love to her right there in the surf. The physical had been hot and heavy, but it had always been about more than sex with Lottie.

"Those kids keep venturing farther and farther out."

Linc looked toward where Lottie was gazing. Four teens were a good distance from the shore, but didn't seem to be in any distress, just swimming and then floating.

He watched them for a few seconds, then put the larger pieces of driftwood he carried into the boat, along with the bag full of smaller pieces. When he returned, he took Lottie's bag, along with the cooler. "Finish packing. I'm going to load this, then we can head to the house to check on Jackie."

Soon her grandmother would be back on her feet. He wouldn't be needed and neither would Lottie. Then she'd be gone, and his life would return to how it had been for the previous twelve years without her.

Why didn't he believe that?

Nothing was ever going to be the same. Now

that he knew how potent her kiss, how bright her smile, how magic her laughter, how could it?

When he returned to where they'd picnicked, Lottie had packed everything except the umbrella base, which she had been unable to pull out of the ground.

"I think it's stuck."

"Let me," he offered. "I drove the base deep to secure it so the wind wouldn't blow it away."

She moved aside, watching as he pulled the umbrella free. "You made that look easy."

"It's all in how you flex the biceps," he teased.

Lowering her lashes, she sent him a tentative smile. "For the record, I like how you flex your biceps, Linc Thomas."

But not enough that she'd stay. He hated that the thought hit him, but it did, and he couldn't shake it. Knowing he owed her an explanation, he searched for words, but her attention had gone beyond him to the water.

"I think those kids are trying to swim to the island. I don't think they should."

Putting the umbrella over his shoulder, Linc glanced toward where the teens had been playing.

She was right. They shouldn't be trying to cross the inlet. The water that had been fairly calm earlier was now choppy. The teen in the back wasn't a very strong swimmer. The others weren't great, but that one was already struggling to keep up.

Hand going to her hip, Lottie frowned with concern. "Have they even thought about the fact that once they make it to the island, they have to cross again to get back to Fripp and the current will be stronger?"

"They'll realize and turn around." Linc hoped so, but wasn't confident enough that he didn't want to keep an eye on them until they'd made it safely to shore.

While Linc pulled up the anchor, Lottie didn't seem able to take her eyes off where the teens were.

"We shouldn't leave until we see what those kids are going to do."

Linc nodded. He hadn't planned to.

"Linc, tell them to turn back." The pitch in Lottie's voice had heightened. "They make me nervous."

"They're not going to hear me over the water." Nor did he expect them to listen. Kids that age felt invincible. He started the boat. "We'll move closer until they make it across."

Once they had, he'd do his best to convince them to accept a ride back to the other side. Hopefully, they'd be smart enough to say yes.

When they'd made it close enough, Linc killed the engine to use the trolley motor to guide the boat closer to the kids so he could pull them into the boat without the wake creating more issues.

"Hey. The water has gotten choppy. You guys want a lift?" he called, but their response was lost on him as the teen farthest away disappeared beneath the water.

One. Two. Three.

Where was he?

"Linc! He's not come up! The one in the back, he's under!" Lottie exclaimed. The teens closest to the boat turned toward where their friend had been.

"Where's Slade?" one asked, looking around at the two friends near him. "He was just here."

"There. There he is," another said as the boy bobbed up only to disappear beneath the murky water again.

"Slade?" they yelled.

Stomach knotting, Linc reached for a life preserver, mentally gauging the distance the current had pulled the boy when he'd popped up, knowing the water could have him anywhere before he could reach him.

Lord, help me with what I'm about to do.

"Call for help, Lottie," he ordered. "Get the others in the boat and call for help."

Realizing what he intended, fear widened Lottie's eyes and she grabbed his arm. "No. You shouldn't go in."

Although logically he knew Lottie was right, that he risked being caught in the current that had the boy, Linc couldn't not go in.

He was that kid's only chance.

No! Lottie wasn't sure if the scream was just in her head or if it had echoed around the islands. Panic seized her throat so tightly she wasn't even sure she was capable of sound.

Linc had kissed her cheek so quickly she questioned if he really had, then he'd dove into the water.

Her instinct was to go after him, to keep the boat so close that she'd be able to get him back aboard. She didn't allow herself to question how she'd do that, just that that's what she wanted to do. But Linc was right. She had to call for help and get the other kids on board first.

Pulling herself together, Lottie shifted her gaze from where Linc's strong breaststrokes cut through the choppy water to the freaked-out teens now clinging to the side of the boat. She had to get them out of the water before there was possibly more than one crisis. Once she had them safe, she'd use the trolley and stayed as close to where Linc swam as she could. He'd be okay. He'd get to the teen and they'd both be just fine.

"There's a ladder I can lower on the other

side," she called down to the teens. "It'll make getting in easier. Can you make it there?"

Staying close to the boat and each other, the trio swam to where Lottie had lowered the ladder into the water and, while making the emergency call, was waiting to help them up.

A male teen climbed into the boat, struggling enough that Lottie was glad she'd gotten them into the boat prior to chasing after Linc. Finally, he was on board.

"You next Jill," he called to the sole female of the group, leaning forward to reach for the girl attempting to climb up the ladder.

She grabbed hold, but her arms wobbled.

"I can't do it, Jeff." Tears mingled with the water droplets running down her face. "I'm scared and can't pull myself out of the water."

"Help her, Trey," the teen told the boy still in the water. "Push her onto the ladder."

Lottie dropped her phone, midcall, onto the boat deck to help reach for the girl.

With Trey's assistance from in the water, Jill scrambled up the ladder enough that Lottie and Jeff were able to grab hold of her and pull her onto the deck by falling back and bringing her with them.

Next, Lottie and Jeff helped get the last teen from the water.

Finally, all three were in the boat.

"Here." Lottie tossed the shivering girl the blanket she and Linc had used for their picnic, then gestured to the boys. "There're towels in that bin."

They said something, but Lottie didn't know what. Heart pounding, lungs screaming, head spinning, she searched the water. "Where's Linc? Where is he?"

There was no sign of him or the missing boy, just the life preserver being carried out toward the sea.

Linc's lungs burned. His muscles ached. At some point during his swim, he'd kicked off his waterlogged shoes, knowing they were slowing him down, but not quite sure how he'd gotten them off as he'd never stopped pushing forward.

He'd caught sight of the kid, not fifteen feet in front of him, and then miraculously, he reached him, only to watch the kid be snatched under and back out of sight.

Feeling the water's greedy fingers tugging at him, Linc gave in, diving as forcefully as he could toward the kid, grabbing hold of his lifeless arm to pull him close, then kicking as hard as he could to free them from the water's hold. That the boy was no longer conscious was a mixed blessing as it was going to take everything Linc had to get them to the surface, if he was even able to. Had the boy been conscious and panicked, attempting to get them free would have been a hundred times worse.

Diving in had been foolish, but he'd known he preferred death over not attempting to rescue the kid. He couldn't do nothing and always wonder what if he'd tried.

But now, as lifesaving air seemed so far away, he wondered if this was the end. With that thought came all the life regrets, all the things he wished he'd said, done. Every thought evolved around Lottie. She filled his mind, his heart.

He loved her, always had, always would. He should have told her. He should have kissed her every chance he'd had and not worried about what the future held. He should have embraced every precious moment during her time in South Carolina. He should have—his mind grew fuzzy. He kicked his legs harder, but they were cold, heavy and didn't seem to be propelling him and the boy forward any longer.

"Linc!" Lottie's cry sliced through the water. "Linc!"

Was he dreaming? Her voice a siren's song playing in his mind, beckoning him to find her. She sounded so close. Keeping his grip on the boy and his focus on where Lottie called him, he broke the surface, gulped air, hacked, coughed, gulped more air as he searched for where her voice came from.

"Linc!" And then, there she was, his beautiful rescuer guiding the boat near and tossing a roped life preserver to him.

Arms like gelatin, fingers numb with cold and gripping the kid so tightly, he struggled to get the life preserver around the boy, but finally managed. Getting him into the boat was going to be a feat, but time was of the essence as the teen still lay lax against him.

Kicking them to the edge of the boat, still gasping to recatch his breath, Linc was able to lift the kid enough to where his friends pulled him into the boat. Lottie leaned forward and extended her hand, obviously thinking she was going to help him. Linc shook his head.

"Start CPR." Talking hurt. He coughed. "Not breathing." Another cough. "CPR."

She glanced into the boat, presumably at the kid, then back at him. "But—"

"CPR now, Lottie." He knew she wanted him out of the water. He also knew that every second the kid wasn't breathing reduced the odds of her getting him back. Linc would be okay, Lottie might not know that, but Linc did. She needed to save the kid. "The others can get me up."

They'd have to. He didn't think he could climb into the boat unassisted if he had to.

* * *

Torn, Lottie knew Linc was right. She had to get CPR started STAT. Trey and Jeff were more capable of pulling Linc into the boat than she was, anyway. But leaving him, taking her eyes off him again when she'd felt such devastation at not being able to find him on the water's surface, felt near impossible.

Pulling the life preserver off the limp kid, Lottie scooted it toward Jeff even as she started checking for Slade's pulse. "Get this to Linc. Use it to pull him onto the boat like we just did for your friend. Now."

Her fingers pressed against Slade's cold skin. No pulse. No surprise. She gave the kid a breath, then another prior to starting compressions. Her arms felt disconnected from the rest of her as her insides trembled. Linc was okay, she assured herself. She had to revive the boy Linc had gone to such great heroic lengths to try to save.

"Come on," she urged, counting the reps in her head between compressions and breaths, as she racked her brain to recall what the exact protocol for resuscitating a drowning victim currently was. She'd never done this! Not on a kid whose lungs had filled with water. "Please. Take a breath."

Lottie focused on her patient rather than on the teens' efforts to get Linc into the boat, but from her periphery she was well aware they still hadn't pulled him into the boat.

Over and over, she compressed the boy's chest, tears streaming down her face, knowing she had to keep going rather than look toward the others to see what was taking so long. Had Linc gone back under? Was that why she hadn't heard the reassuring thud of him landing on the boat's deck?

"Lord, please. Please. Please. Please," she whispered, continuing her deep compressions to the boy's chest.

Sputter. Water spewed from the boy's mouth. Cough.

"He's alive! Slade's alive!" Jill exclaimed, distracting the other teens from their rescue efforts of pulling Linc into the boat. Fortunately, he was finally in enough that he tumbled onto the deck and Lottie heard that reassuring thud of a landing.

Thank you, God.

Lottie fought the urge to abandon her post to rush to Linc, but knew Slade wasn't out of the woods so kept up her efforts on him, pressing deeply on his chest.

He had a pulse. A weak one, but it was there.

"Do not ever do that again."

From where Linc sat in the back of the ambulance, a blanket wrapped around him to fight off his chill despite the summer heat, he eyed where Lottie clenched his hand so tightly that he might have bruises.

"It worked out."

"But it might not have." She squeezed his hand even tighter, then lifted it to press his fingers against her chest. Her warmth seeped into him, abating some of the chill that he'd begun to think would never subside. "Do you have any idea how scared I was that I'd lost you when I couldn't spot you anywhere?"

"I'm sorry I scared you, Lottie." He'd been scared himself. Terrified. "I'm fine." Part of him still couldn't believe he'd made it out of the water. When he closed his eyes, he could still feel the darkness pulling him under, making his lungs burn for air. He inhaled sharply, appreciating the reassuring air filling his lungs. "I'm just waiting for these guys to tell me I can leave so we can go home."

"Dude, she's right," said the paramedic who had given him a once-over as he came back over to the truck from where he'd been speaking with a sheriff's deputy. "You shouldn't have dived in."

Lottie's look said, *see!*

"But it would be a much different story here

today if you hadn't," the emergency worker continued, his voice full of gratitude.

"The kid's going to be okay?"

"He'd regained consciousness by the time my buddies got him loaded into their ambulance. He didn't remember you or how he got out of the water, but he asked about his friends, wanting to know if they were okay."

"That's a good sign." Lottie breathed hard, still clutching Linc's hand as if she might never let go. "Hopefully, he won't have any brain damage from having been without oxygen."

"They didn't think so. He could answer their questions and his neuro check seemed okay."

"Good." Linc let the medic go through another unnecessary neuro check on him. "I'm fine, too, just ready to go home."

"Let me have you sign some papers and then we'll release you." The man slapped Linc on the shoulder. "Thanks for what you did out there, man. You're a hero."

"Gram was all hyped up over what happened this afternoon, but she is finally asleep," Lottie said when she came back into the living room and saw Linc was awake and sitting up on the sofa.

"Unlike me who slept most of the evening." Linc shook his head. "Crazy. I never nap."

Moving the blanket she'd put over him, she sat down next to him, scooting as close as she could without climbing into his lap. "You never almost drown, either."

Linc's arm went around her and she felt his face nuzzling into her hair. "Thank you for staying by my side while the paramedic checked me, Lottie."

She leaned back enough to look at him. "Are you kidding? You thought I was going to leave? Linc, if you ever scare me like that again, I—"

He placed his fingers over her lips. "It's okay. Everything is okay. I'm fine. Slade is being kept overnight for observation but is expected to be released in the morning. Everything, everyone, is fine."

"I'm not fine, Linc. Not in the slightest." Lottie wiggled to where she could palm his cheeks and make him look directly at her. "Please do not ever, ever, scare me that way again."

Smiling, Linc stared into her eyes. "Yes, ma'am. You've made your point."

"Why are you smiling? I'm serious, Linc. This isn't funny. You really, really scared me."

He reached up and took her hand into his, lacing their fingers. "Why wouldn't I be smiling? I'm alive, Lottie, and the most beautiful woman I've ever known is beside me. I'm allowed to smile." When she started to say something, he gave her hand a reassuring squeeze and continued, "What I did was foolish. I know that. But I can't say I'm sorry." His hand trembled where it held hers. "I just can't."

Realizing what he meant, she sighed. "I understand. I was just so scared and...have I told you lately how wonderful you are?"

Lifting her fingers to his lips, he pressed a kiss there, sending butterflies dancing in her stomach. "Tell me."

She stared into his eyes, her own a bit glassy. "You're wonderful."

With that, she pressed her lips to his in a soft kiss. "Wonderful," she repeated, dropping more kisses over his lips, his face. She'd thought she'd lost him and that was unacceptable. No matter what happened between them, no matter what the future held, she needed to know Linc was somewhere in the world, making it a better place.

"You doing that is wonderful."

She kissed him again. This time, longer, more fully as she scooted closer and he kissed her back. They kissed until Lottie was as air hungry as if she'd been the one under water, until her heart pounded so hard she thought it might burst in her chest.

Soon kisses weren't enough. She needed more, to feel the life within him, within her.

By the way Linc tugged at her shirt hem, she guessed he needed more, too.

Her shirt disappeared, as did his. Kisses turned to touches turned to more kisses.

"You saved me out there today," he whispered against her skin. "It was your voice I heard calling to me like that of Lorelei, only luring me back to the surface and to you rather than to my doom."

Lottie didn't want to think about the water. Not anymore. Not ever again. She just wanted to feel all the magic Linc stirred inside her, to embrace that and him.

That's just what she did.

Sunbeams broke through the darkness of Lottie's room, waking her. The events of the day before rushed through her mind. Linc! She opened her eyes, took in that she was in her bed. So was Linc. Safe. Alive. Warm against her bare body.

"You're here," she whispered, not quite believing how they'd spent much of the night.

Linc's eyes opened. Staring sleepily at her, concern flooded his blue gaze. "Do you want me to leave?"

She shook her head. "No." Her mind was full of questions, but that wasn't one of them. She wanted him right where he was. Next to her. "This certainly complicates things, though."

The worst part was, she wasn't sure she cared how complicated their having had sex made things. All she'd cared about was that Linc was alive. As if needing to reassure herself, she placed her palm against him, feeling the strong beat of his heart, watching the rise and fall of his chest.

"This only complicates things as much as we let it." He lifted her hand to his lips and pressed a kiss to her fingertips. "We don't have to rush things, Lottie."

She laughed. "Too late. We did that last night."

He scooted up onto his elbow. "Maybe, but maybe it's okay if we don't overthink this. I know you're going back to Boston in a couple of weeks. That what happened yesterday upset you and maybe that's why last night happened. I have no regrets and I don't want you to, either."

"I don't regret last night." How could she when his making love to her had surpassed her most erotic fantasy? Their first time had been hot and heavy, but when they'd gone to her room, every touch had been as if his sole purpose for living was to give her pleasure. He had. Oh, so much pleasure.

Remembering had her stirring in places that should be too sore to stir.

"Why don't we just enjoy what's left of our

summer reunion?" he suggested. "We'll figure things out when our time is up."

"Sounds simple enough." But Lottie knew better. She knew how difficult leaving was going to be. She'd done it before and spent twelve years missing him. How much more difficult would leaving be this time knowing the deep ache that awaited her at his absence? An ache she suspected would far surpass what her teenaged heart had felt.

"I can see the indecision on your face, hear it in your words." He cupped her face, looked straight into her eyes. "Lottie, if you'd rather me leave and us pretend that last night never happened, then I'll leave. But don't ask me to pretend that *we* didn't happen because I won't. We happened. We happened twelve years ago, and we happened again this summer."

"I don't want you to leave, and I don't want to pretend we didn't happen. I couldn't if I tried." She wasn't that skilled an actress.

"And last night?"

"Last night happened." She took a deep breath. "I wanted last night to happen."

Linc's grin might be the most beautiful thing she'd ever seen. "Then it's okay if I kiss you good morning?"

Swallowing, she nodded. "More than okay."

She wanted his good morning kiss. Now and

forever. She had now and was going to embrace it with welcoming arms, embrace Linc with open arms.

Forever would have to take care of itself.

CHAPTER TEN

"I DON'T WANT to go into the water."

From where he trod calm water just off Pritchard's, Linc eyed where Lottie sat on the side of the boat and knew exactly how she felt. Going in that first time after their rescue hadn't been easy. He'd done so the very day he'd awakened in Lottie's bed. He'd had to. He'd had to wash away the remnants of fear that hit when he'd gone home, stepped out on to his back deck and felt dread at the gentle waves rolling in rather than the healthy respect he'd always afforded the sea. It hadn't been easy, but he'd made himself go in. Just as claustrophobia and panic were hitting, making him think he was going to get sucked under, he hadn't. He'd swam long enough to erase the hesitation that was similar to what was gripping Lottie now. And he'd purposely swam every day since. On several occasions, Lottie had watched from the shore, refusing to get into the water during their nightly watch the sunset "date."

He splashed water her way, the droplets soaking into the red material of her bikini. "I should have made you go in last week."

She shook her head. "There's nowhere that says I have to go in ever again."

"You love the water."

She shrugged. "Things change."

He imagined that's exactly what would happen when she left Fripp, but for now, she was there and he was determined to replace her fear with respect and her bad memories with good ones. In the process, he'd do the same for himself. He'd certainly been making good memories the past week. With Lottie.

"I won't let anything happen to you. Come in and swim with me."

Eyeing him, she sighed. "You're going to make me do this even though I don't want to, aren't you?"

"It's for your own good."

"Fine, but I don't like you very much right now." Sighing again, she pinched her nose and slid off into the water. Linc was by her side within seconds, but let her surface on her own, wanting her to regain her confidence in the water. She flung her hair back, then blinked the water away from her eyes. "Happy now?"

Wrapping his arms around her waist, he kept them afloat with little kicks of his legs. "I've not quit being happy since this beautiful cardiologist rescued me."

His comment had her expression softening. She curved her arms around his neck and her legs linked at his waist. "Tell me more."

"Once upon a time there was this woman," he began. "She came to the island to visit with her sick grandmother. While there, she ran into—"

"The big, bad wolf?" Lottie's eyes twinkled, and he could feel her body relaxing against his.

Laughing, he shook his head. "Although she's wearing a really hot red bathing suit, her name isn't Red. Now, quit interrupting."

"I think a fish just nibbled at my toes, but okay, I won't interrupt."

"She ran into this really awesome physical therapist who helped her grandmother." Linc paused. "Did a fish really just bite your toes?"

She fluttered her lashes. "Maybe." Her legs squeezed his waist. "I definitely felt something."

"Let me check your toes."

Still clinging to his neck, Lottie straightened from where her legs had been wrapped around him and raised her foot out of the water. "See?"

"Looks okay to me."

"How can you tell from that far away?"

"I'm pretty close," he pointed out, not seeing anything wrong with her toes.

With a sudden swivel of her body, Lottie splashed him. Hard. Then laughing, she took off swimming as hard as she could toward the beach.

"I'm going to get you for that," he warned, chasing after her. He could have caught her within seconds but let her get close enough to the shore that they could stand prior to grabbing her leg and pulling her to him. "Hello, there."

Laughing, she splashed him again. "That took longer than I thought it would."

"You wanted me to catch you?"

Wrapping her arms back around his neck, she smiled at him. "Absolutely. Why wouldn't I?"

"Because of this." He dunked them both under the water that was thankfully fairly clear and kissed her, letting his air be hers and vice versa.

They stayed under until Linc's lungs cried for him to surface, but Lottie held on just a little longer, her tongue slipping into his mouth.

When they surfaced, he grabbed her hand. "Come on. We're going back to the boat."

"What? Why?" But her eyes danced with mischief. She knew exactly why.

"We're going to my place for more water therapy." Still, holding her hand and loving the sound of her laughter, he kicked off the sandy bottom and, taking her with him, swam toward the boat. "This time in my shower."

"Swim faster, Linc. Swim faster."

"I can't believe you're leaving."

Lottie zipped her suitcase closed and eyed where her grandmother sat on her bed, watching her. "You knew I was leaving, Gram. I was only here until you were back on your feet, which you are. Dr. Collins was so impressed at your last appointment."

"Who knew being impressive was a bad thing? I could fake another break if it meant you could stay longer." Gram sighed. "You've said goodbye to Linc?"

In some ways, it felt as if they'd been saying goodbye every moment since Dr. Collins had released Gram to start walking on her boot and Lottie had set a date to return to Boston. With the countdown on, they'd squeezed out every moment, Linc even opting to take a few vacation days to extend their time together.

Lottie bit into her lower lip. "Not yet. We'll say our goodbyes when he drives me to the airport."

"You're a fool to leave him."

"I know." She was. Yet, she couldn't stay. Sighing, she plopped onto the bed next to her grandmother. "I have to go back to Boston,

Gram. I have a contract, a life. And I like my life there, but the truth is, I like my life here, too. I wish I could stuff you both into my suitcase and take you with me."

"I'd never be happy away from the island, but I am going to miss you." Gram let out a long breath. "I understand that you have to do what you have to do. Just be sure you say the things you need to say to the person you need to say them to, too."

When Linc arrived, Lottie hugged her grandmother a thousand times and shed close to that many tears. More. "I love you, Gram. Keep doing your therapy and I'll be back to visit at Christmas, sooner if I can."

Christmas, she thought as Linc crossed the bridge leading onto Sea Island Parkway. Christmas felt an eternity away. Maybe she'd be able to pull a few long weekends prior to then. She glanced over at Linc. Would he want to see her when she came back? The past few weeks had been so amazing, but then, they'd done amazing before.

Her stomach clenched. They'd danced all around.

Linc was mostly silent as they headed toward the airport. How could he appear so calm when she felt anything but?

"This isn't easy," she admitted, swiping at her leaky eyes again.

"Goodbyes are never easy."

Lottie's breath caught. "Is that what this is? Are we saying goodbye again, Linc?"

If not for the way he white-knuckled the steering wheel, Lottie might have thought he hadn't heard her. That he didn't immediately answer spoke volumes. Hurt and anger erupted within her. She was doing what she had to do. Did she matter so little that he'd rather say goodbye than to make a long-distance relationship work?

"Is my question such a difficult one to answer?"

He stared straight ahead. "Is goodbye what you want this to be?"

"You know it isn't."

"What do you suggest? That we see each other when you can sneak away to South Carolina for us to pick back up as if you'd never left?"

"I know it's not ideal, but would that be so bad?"

He sighed. "I guess we'll find out. I'm not willing to spend the next twelve years wishing we'd tried."

Relief filled her. Linc wasn't saying goodbye forever.

"I'll schedule time off to come back. A long weekend in September, maybe, but definitely longer in October." Christmas was definitely too long. "Do you think you could come to Boston at Thanksgiving? I can introduce you to my friends, especially Camilla. I've told her all about you."

His jaw flexed. "A long weekend in a couple of months, a few days in October, and I'll request time off to come to you in November."

"I'll be on call at Christmas but plan to take off the week after. Maybe we can work it to where we'll see each other most months."

He let out a long breath. "Why do I feel as if we're back to where we were twelve years ago? Saying goodbye on a relationship high, but destined to have time and distance pull us apart?"

Lottie's chest hurt. "That's not going to happen. Not for me." She swallowed the lump in her throat. "Is that what you expect to happen on your end?"

"I don't think I'm going to enjoy you being a literal thousand miles away, if that's what you're asking."

"What I'm asking is if you believe in our relationship? Because if you do and I do, then time and distance shouldn't be able to pull us apart."

He hesitated, then asked, "Do you see yourself ever moving to Fripp?"

Lottie thought about his question. "In theory it sounds great, but I have a contract with the hospital in Boston. I enjoy my job and being a part of the research team that helps develop new lifesaving technologies."

He took a deep breath that had her feeling defensive.

"What about you? Do you see yourself ever moving to Boston?"

To his credit he didn't immediately answer but seemed to soul search his answer. "No, Lottie, I don't."

"I— Okay." She rubbed the sudden throbbing at her temple. "It's okay. We don't have to figure everything out right now. We will make this work." Somehow.

Lottie was still telling herself that when Linc pulled the car up to the airport departure's curb, put the car gear into park then got out to get her suitcase.

"Call me when you land in Boston."

"As soon as we taxi in. I love you, Linc."

"Lottie, you tell me that now? When you're leaving me?"

"I don't know what to say to make this better, Linc. My heart is breaking to leave you and yet I have to go."

He studied her a moment, then nodded. "I know you do. It's what was always going to happen."

He sounded so resigned to their fate that Lottie couldn't stand not touching him a moment longer so she threw her arms around him, kissing him while she still could.

When he pulled back, he cupped her face, stared into her eyes for a long moment, then kissed her with such intensity that Lottie had to quell the urge to jump back into his car and forget about Boston and everything else.

As much as she told herself that he wasn't kissing her goodbye, old doubts plagued that that's exactly what he was doing. That once she was back in Boston, he'd shut her out yet again, and she was destined for the worst heartbreak of her life.

"You're not coming to South Carolina?" Hoping he'd misheard, Linc clicked up his phone's volume to be sure whatever Lottie said came across loud and clear above the ocean's roar.

When her call had come through, he'd stepped outdoors and onto his back deck. Moonlight reflected off the water, highlighting the whitecaps crashing onto the shoreline. From the point they'd realized a September trip home wasn't going to happen, they'd been counting down the days until this weekend.

"It's not that I don't want to, but we've been so slammed. The hospital administrator and my coworkers were so good to me during Gram's recovery that I can't just leave them hanging."

"But you're okay with leaving me hanging?" His question was as much for himself as to her. They talked on the phone most days, but those calls weren't as long or frequent as they'd been when she first left. He'd told himself he understood when she canceled in September, but now she was doing so again. He'd gotten a leave authorized in November, but would she end up canceling on him? Citing that she wouldn't be able to get off work anyway?

"It's not like that." Her frustration came over the phone line. "You know it's not. I miss you."

"Just not enough to make coming back a priority?" Gripping the phone, he ran his other fingers through his hair. More and more he felt the distance between them. Had she gone back to Boston and realized he'd been nothing more than a summer fling? A reunion with her past?

"Airplanes fly in both directions."

He grimaced. She was right. He'd checked flights dozens of times, but something always held him back from booking one. He'd been at the hospital for less than a year, but he had some time accumulated and could shuffle his schedule. For that matter, he could go for a few days most weeks. So why hadn't he? Instead, he'd thrown himself into the remodel, working late into the night. It's what he'd been doing when his phone had rung so she could cancel yet again. He'd been excited to see her, to show her his progress on the house, which he'd finished much sooner than he'd originally planned. Why? As an added lure for her to come back to South Carolina? If he wasn't enough, did he really think finishing the remodel of the house she loved would make a difference?

"Linc? Are you still there?"

"I'm here."

She hesitated, then asked, "Just not answering me?"

"I don't know what to say, Lottie."

"The right thing would be to say that you understand and that if not before, you'll see me when you come here in November."

In her big city glitzy world where he wouldn't fit in and she'd see the stark differences between them. Sure, he'd gotten his degree, but working at the hospital in Beaufort wasn't the same as cavorting with her Harvard friends.

"I really don't like the cold."

She hesitated, then asked, "Are you saying you're not coming in November?"

Was that what he was saying? Linc leaned against the railing, stared out at the whitecaps breaking against the shore, breathed in the salty ocean air. He missed her, but ever since she'd left, every doubt he'd ever had had surfaced. He'd even relived his conversation with her mother during several dreams that had left him waking in a sweat. Was this really how he wanted to live his life?

"I don't know."

More silence, then, anger spiking in her tone, she said, "Are you so upset with me that you want to fight, Linc? Is that what you're doing? I'm sorry I had to cancel last month. I'm sorry I have to cancel this month. I was unexpectedly off work for six weeks this summer—six weeks!—and in your world, so it's a little difficult for me to get away from mine again so soon."

His world. Her world. Her mother had been right to point out that difference all those years ago. Hadn't he acknowledged that he was an escape for Lottie? Was that the real problem? That he worried outside of their fairy-tale beach paradise that she wouldn't want him? That she'd realize he wasn't so great when thrown into the world she thrived in? He was just existing day by day, cherishing each call, but deep down, waiting for the ax to drop.

"I don't want to fight."

"That's it? That's all you have to say?" Her tone was accusatory. "Work with me here, Linc. At least a little."

He closed his eyes, letting the roar of the ocean sound around him. The wind had picked up, stinging his skin and whipping at his clothes, hair and the phone he pressed to his ear. For so long he'd dreamed of this, living on Fripp. Here he was with his bare feet planted on the deck of that dream and rather than experience the joy he'd once felt, he lived phone call to phone call. What kind of life was that?

He'd let her go all those years ago. It had been the right thing to do. He hadn't needed her mother to tell him that. If it hadn't been the right thing, he'd have gone after her, right?

Or maybe not, because deep down he'd wondered if Vivien had been right about her other claim, too.

My daughter may think she's in love with you because of your little island romance, but that kind of love never holds up when put to the test in the real world. You're both young and share an attraction, but that will fade, and when it does, Lottie will move on to someone more suited for her. Don't ruin her life in the meantime.

Linc's stomach twisted into knots and, curling his fingers, he tapped his fist against a deck post. Not a punch, but hard enough it stung. "I can't do this anymore."

"Do what?" Her pitch had gone up several octaves.

"Be in a long-distance relationship. I just can't. Phone calls and I-miss-yous just aren't enough. I thought I could do this, that they'd be enough, but they're just not. I'm sorry."

Lottie unlocked her apartment door and flicked on the light.

"Oh! Sorry," she said, apologizing to the couple who jumped apart from where they'd been making out on the sofa. "I wasn't thinking, or I'd have made more noise, jiggled my keys or something."

Not that her roommate and ex-boyfriend were likely to have heard her no matter if she'd stamped her feet and beat on the door. Who knew that when she'd removed herself from the picture that Camilla would acknowledge the attraction she'd apparently felt for years, but had kept tamped down out of love of their friendship? How had Lottie missed what was so obvious? Once Camilla had been convinced Lottie truly wasn't getting back together with Brian, she'd asked permission to go for it. Lottie had given her blessing. Regardless of anything between her and Linc, she and Brian weren't right for each other. She loved him, but wasn't in love with him, nor him with her.

Not once had he ever looked at her the way he did at the woman straightening her clothes while simultaneously slapping his hands away. Yeah, Brian had never been like that with her.

"Sorry," Camilla said, a blush staining her tan cheeks. "We were headed out to eat, but then got distracted and…do you want to go with us? We were thinking of hitting that Irish pub over by the Charles that everyone at the hospital has been raving about."

Lottie shook her head. "I'm going to shower and numb my brain with mindless television while vegging out on the sofa."

Her roommate winced. "You still haven't heard from him?"

Fighting the emotions that clawed their way up her throat anytime she thought of Linc, which was often, Lottie shook her head.

"Have you tried calling him?"

She shook her head again. How many times had she started to press his number, but been unable to complete the call? Enough that just thinking about it had hands tightening around her throat. Because what if she called and he didn't answer?

What if she called and his number had been disconnected as he'd done in the past?

She wasn't calling. Much better to not know than to hear that monotonous message about reaching a number that had been disconnected or was no longer in service. Phone calls and I-miss-yous weren't enough. He was right about that. But not having those phone calls and I-miss-yous was tearing her apart.

Why hadn't he called her? How could he have just thrown them away? Being apart wasn't easy, but at least she'd been trying.

Had she really?

Or had she acquiesced too easily when Greg Abbott had asked her if she could cancel her trip to help cover staffing issues? She could have said no and she hadn't. Why not? She'd accused him of purposely wanting to fight, but had she been the one instigating issues?

Camilla hugged her and Brian did, too. "You're sure you don't want to go? Or if you wanted, we could call for takeout and numb our brains along with you."

"Please don't." She shooed them toward the door. "Go. Have fun."

It took a few minutes to convince them that she truly was fine and that in her case, misery did not love company, but eventually they left. Lottie showered, put on her favorite pajamas and curled up on the sofa with a bowl of cereal and the remote control. She clicked on the television. A dog food commercial played on the tele-

242 HEART DOCTOR'S SUMMER REUNION

vision and a big golden dog loped across the screen. Longing tore at Lottie.

"You know it's bad when I even miss Maritime," she mumbled as tears began rolling down her cheeks. She loved her life in Boston, but since coming back, nothing felt the same. Nothing. Not her love for her job. Not her joy in spending time with her friends. Nothing.

She wasn't the same.

She'd left her heart in South Carolina, so how could she expect to love anywhere else?

Which meant what exactly? She had another eight months on her contract with the hospital. She couldn't just up and leave. She didn't even want to.

She'd been the one to call Linc last time, the one to pour her heart out only to be ignored. She'd poured her heart out again, and he'd essentially said what she could give him wasn't enough. Did he expect her to give up her life without him making any concessions so their relationship could work? She wanted a partnership, not someone who couldn't meet her in the middle.

Which meant what? That she no longer wanted Linc? That wasn't right, either. She wanted Linc. She wanted her phone to ring and it to be him telling her how sorry he was that he hadn't called and that he'd need her to pick him up from Logan airport Thanksgiving week.

But she was angry that Linc wasn't putting as much effort into making things work as she'd been.

The commercial ended and the romantic comedy playing came back on. Lottie clicked it off, but the next channel was even worse with an on-screen couple declaring their everlasting love to each other, then embracing.

She clicked the station again and a Celtics came on. Good. Nothing romantic about a basketball game.

Was that what she wanted? Romance?

"I want what Mom and Dad had," she said to the empty room. "They loved each other beyond everything else. I want a love like that."

But her parents had met in college, fell in love and married the summer after they'd graduated. They'd lived in the right neighborhood, socialized with the right people, enjoyed the same things, and wanted a similar life for her. Only, when her mother was planning Lottie's life, she'd missed the key ingredient to her happiness. Vivien had loved Lottie's dad and he'd loved her. Without that, none of the other things mattered. They were just meaningless fluff.

Bored with the ball game, she clicked the channel again and groaned. Seriously? Then again, maybe there were advantages to marrying at first sight.

She glanced at her phone. "Ring." Nothing. "Just ring, okay? Is that too much to ask?"

She picked up a throw pillow, clutched it to her, then buried her face in it to muffle a scream. "Argh!"

Her doorbell rang, and she about jumped out of her skin.

"Lottie?" a voice that might be a hallucination called. "Are you okay?"

Linc had been standing outside Lottie's apartment for longer than he cared to admit. You'd think he'd have had plenty of time to figure out what he wanted to say over the past few days and even during his flight. Apparently not, because he'd gotten there and gotten cold feet that had nothing to do with the twenty degree temperature drop from when he'd left South Carolina.

Lottie's roommate must have thought he had something great to say because when she'd spotted him on the sidewalk as she'd been coming out of the apartment building, she'd done a double take, recognizing him from Lottie's photos, introduced herself and the guy with her, then buzzed him up to their apartment.

"The rest is up to you," she'd said. "If you

can't convince her to open the door, you've no one to blame but yourself."

He hadn't been able to argue that, but he'd meant what he'd said to Lottie. Phone calls and I-miss-yous weren't enough. Not nearly so.

He might not be enough either, but he was here to find out, to try his best to be the man she needed him to be.

But standing outside her door, he wondered if he should have given her a heads-up. What if she turned him away? What if he'd blown it with her again because he'd been too cowardly to trust in her feelings for him? To trust in *them*?

Then she'd screamed.

"Let me in, Lottie." He knocked on the door, again. This time louder, more insistent. "It's Linc."

The door swung open. Eyeing him, she crossed her arms over her cartoon-character-covered pajama top. Blocking the doorway, she tapped her foot. "You think I didn't recognize your voice? I mean, you haven't called, but it's only been three days since you told me you didn't want to do this anymore."

Yep, she was mad.

"Can I come inside?"

She moved aside, allowing him to come into her apartment. He looked around at the modern white-and-gray style. The only thing that looked familiar was the twisted wire and drift-wood lamp next to her sofa. He focused on Jackie's art, drawing strength from the bit of South Carolina in the room.

"We need to talk."

"Really?" She arched her brow. "Is that why you haven't called for the past three days?"

Less than thirty seconds and she'd already thrown that at him twice. Not good, but then, had he expected otherwise? Did he even deserve otherwise?

"If I'd called, I'd have said things I didn't want to say," he began, hoping he could make her understand. Walking over to the lamp, he ran his finger over the driftwood. "Some things need to be said in person."

"What things?" She crossed her arms again, probably to protect her heart from the likes of him. Taking in her colorful cartoon pajamas, clipped-up blond hair, fresh face, and bare feet with their orange and black polish, Linc's heart swelled.

"Things like I miss you and phone calls that aren't enough."

She snorted. "I think you said that loud and clear the other night."

"Then you agree?"

"What do you want me to say, Linc? If I say yes, then it means I'm acknowledging that we aren't working and I'm not willing to do that. If you are, then why are you here?"

"It's not us that's not working, Lottie," he pointed out. "We'd be working just fine if we were together to be working."

"I can't leave Boston, Linc."

"I'm not asking you to."

Lower lip trembling, she looked at him in disbelief and with a light in her eyes that she might start throwing things his way. "You came all this way to end things with me in person? That's what you couldn't tell me over the phone? Seriously? Just leave now."

"I came all this way because I'm not willing to risk things ending," he said.

She blinked. "I don't understand."

"You told me that the airlines flew both ways. That hit close to home. Closer than I've ever revealed to you. I should have already been here, Lottie, but I was afraid to."

"Afraid to? Now I'm really lost. You're the bravest person I've ever known."

He shook his head. "I'm not brave, Lottie. Not when it comes to you." He took her hands in his, marveling at their warmth. "I should have come after you last time. There were reasons I didn't, but those reasons don't apply anymore. Not really."

"What reasons?"

How much should he tell her? Everything. She needed to know the truth. Yet, he didn't want to blame someone else for his own short-comings. He'd let Lottie's mom influence how he'd handled things. Because he'd believed her when she'd told him that he'd ruin Lottie's life for nothing more than a summer romance that hadn't fizzled itself out yet, and thinking himself altruistic, he'd cut off all ties. In reality, Vivien's words had played into his own deeply held belief that he wasn't good enough for her and that once she left Fripp, she'd realize that their summer had been nothing more than a fantasy. He'd spent the past twelve years trying to make himself into someone good enough.

When push had come to shove, he'd still not felt good enough.

"Your mother loved you with all her heart, Lottie. She knew how much being a cardiologist meant to you and she recognized that I was a threat to that dream."

Pulling her hands free, Lottie studied him. "You were never a threat to me."

"Had I let you come back to South Carolina, I'd have destroyed your dream and eventually your feelings for me."

Clasping her fingers together, she gasped. "That's not true."

"You'd have thrown away your scholarship.

As infatuated as I was, I at least recognized that I couldn't let you do that."

Lottie's color heightened, and she shook her head in denial of what he was saying. "If I opted to come back to South Carolina, that was my decision to make. Not hers."

"Maybe not, but it was mine to make sure that I wasn't the reason you threw everything away. I told myself that if how you felt about me was real, then it would still be real when you finished university."

Her eyes filled with accusation. "You didn't answer my call, Linc. I poured my heart out to you and you changed your phone number. How could you do that? Why would you do that?"

"That's where the true cowardice comes in." And this was where the truth came out. "Had I not changed my number, I'd have given in to calling you back, Lottie. I got rid of my phone and all the numbers in it so that I couldn't do that. I couldn't be the reason you didn't achieve your dreams."

She drew in a ragged breath. "You hurt me so badly."

"I know." Oh, how he knew and how he wished he could take that pain away. "There's more."

"More?"

"Your mom convincing me to let you go was

easy, because deep down I never believed I deserved your love. I never believed I was good enough for someone like you to love someone like me."

Lottie looked at him in confusion. "Someone like you? You're the best man I've ever known. How could you not be good enough? Any woman would be lucky to have you."

He shrugged. "I've only ever wanted one, and she was way out of my league."

"Why do you keep saying that? Did I ever give you the impression I thought you were beneath me?"

He shook his head.

"It was Mama, wasn't it? You don't have to answer. I know it was." Lottie took a deep breath. "It took me a long time to understand why she and Gram didn't get along, but it's because of that. Mama's love of high society and living a life others envied. She had this vision of how my life was supposed to be and it blinded her to the truth, even when Gram pointed it out to her, which I'm sure she did and that that was the source of their bickering."

"I don't want to say anything derogatory about your mother, Lottie. She loved you, and I've no doubt there wasn't anything she wouldn't have done for you if she believed it was in your best interest."

"That doesn't excuse her interfering in my life to the extend she did. For so long I stayed with Brian because I knew it's what she wanted… It took me much too long to realize that it was up to me to live my life and to make my own choices." She narrowed her gaze. "Why are you here, Linc?"

He sucked in a deep breath. "To tell you I'm sorry I broke your heart twelve years ago."

"That's it?" Her fingers curled into fists at her sides. "You're sorry you broke my heart?"

"I want to make it up to you, if you'll let me." He knew he'd hurt her. He also knew she was worth putting his heart on the line.

"How can you make up for twelve years of nursing a broken heart, Linc?"

"By making sure that the next twelve fill your heart so full it overflows into the next twelve and the twelve after that and so forth." Linc's heart pounded so hard it made keeping air in his lungs impossible. "I'm going to sell my place on Fripp and move to Boston to be near you, Lottie."

Her eyes rounded. "No. You can't do that. You love that house and Fripp."

"I love you more."

Lottie suspected she'd fallen asleep during the marrying a stranger show, was dreaming, and would awaken to Camilla returning any moment. But until that happened, she was going with this dream. Because Linc saying I love you to her was the ultimate dream. One that had her heart flopping around like a fish on Gram's dock.

"You love me?"

"I have always loved you, Charlotte Fairwell. I always will."

"I'm going to wrap my arms around you and tell you how happy I am that you're here, that I love you, too, and if there's nothing there but air and I wake up, I'm going to cry," she told him, still thinking she had to be dreaming. "Please be real."

"I'm real." He took her hands into his again, holding them as if they were the most precious things he'd ever held. "So very real that I worry you'll find me dull outside our Fripp fairy tale."

"Never," she whispered, pulling her hands free to hug him tightly to her and pressing her face against his chest. "Fripp isn't the fairy tale. You are."

"I hope so because I don't ever want to go back to being without you. If that means living where it's cold, then so be it."

"I'll keep you warm." She hugged him tighter. "Until I've fulfilled my contract and we can go to Fripp, I'll keep you warm."

"We don't have to go there, Lottie."

"I miss Gram and Maritime."

"She misses you, too. Jackie says Maritime sits outside your bedroom door and whines."

Imagining the dog doing that, Lottie laughed. "Now I know I'm dreaming."

"She loves you and so do I. We don't have to make any definite plans tonight, Lottie. We can stay here or go to Fripp or to Timbuktu so long as we're together."

"Sounds perfect."

"Almost. I don't want to rush things, but we've wasted so much time already that I don't want to be apart any longer." He reached into his pocket and pulled out Gram's wedding band. "Oops. Wrong one."

Lottie's breath caught as she watched him dig back into his pocket and pull out the other half of Gram's wedding ring set.

"When I asked for her permission to do what I'm about to do, she insisted I take these." Linc knelt on one knee. "Marry me, Lottie. Tonight. Tomorrow. Next week or a year from now. Whenever you're sure I'm the one you want to spend your life with, marry me."

Choking back tears, Lottie nodded. "How could I say no to a man with an ocean view on Fripp?"

He laughed. "Guess I can let Jackie know I

won't be auditioning for that marrying someone I don't know show, after all."

"Definitely not. You're my real-life fairy-tale happy-ever-after."

"Ditto."

* * * * *